THE LOST PETAL

of the

WHITE ROSE

GRANT WINSTON

Print ISBN: 978-1-54392-672-9

eBook ISBN: 978-1-54392-673-6

This is a work of fiction. Names, characters, places, and incidents either are the product of the author's imagination or are used fictitiously, and any resemblance to actual persons, living or dead, business establishments, events, or locales is entirely coincidental.

CHAPTER 1

Melibea Paz, Ph.D. turned graduate assistant, sat in the university's planetarium, as she had most days and nights for more than eight months, peering into the data and images produced from her prescribed search of an area in a distant galaxy, more than 340 million light years from Earth, trying to find a cosmic needle in a haystack—an early stage supernova. This night was a late night session for Melibea. During each of those previous nights she had seen countless very beautiful stars. But on none of those nights had she seen the elusive early stage Type 1a, or even a potential Type 1ax, mini-supernova, or any other type. She was saddened, and desponded that her search was as ill-fated as those made by yesteryear's explorers in their failed searches to discover the fabled Northwest Passage. She had been so initially encouraged by her target area of this particular galaxy, an older galaxy that most astronomers thought came to be after two earlier galaxies had merged and spun around and around together, and then produced a thousands-of-light-years-wide beauty that was beautiful eons before Earth had seen the light of its own days.

What, she had asked herself, could be more exciting than her very own discovery of a supernova; a discombobulated star, or two partnered stars, perturbed enough to create a gigantic thermonuclear explosion? Now that extraterrestrial life, primitive, but life nevertheless, had already been confirmed on at least six, and some scientists were prepared to say seven, exoplanets, a supernova would do nicely.

From the radio, the voice of the public broadcaster with the sibilant "s" droned on about the latest mutations of vestigial American democracy.

"Meanwhile it is expected that today the WWP Democratic Party will announce that WWP has once again been awarded naming rights of the party with the high bid estimated to be somewhere north of 17 billion dollars. That would be a bargain basement price compared to the naming rights awarded last week to IMC by the IMC Republican Party. That award was given for the IMC bid of just over 31 billion dollars. . . . .

Melibea was again up late night hours, using the data and images returned not from the state university's own impressive telescopes, but from the recently activated Henrietta Leavett telescope, which had joined her senior, but more technologically limited partner, Hubble telescope, parked outside of Earth. While amateur astronomers could still access the Hubble, the consortium of benefactors, some of the most important ones from Mel's own university, who developed and shot up the Henrietta Leavett, made sure it would be dedicated to academia as the primary beneficiary. Mel, as she was affectionately known-- and affection for Mel was fairly widespread—was now 35, with a goal of a second Ph.D., this time in Astronomy. She'd already bagged her B.S. in her second field, and was now behind the plow at the university, which also happened to be a university with one of the most renowned Astronomy and Astrophysics Departments in the United States, if not the world.

Her prior academic love, Botany, had led her to a successful doctoral dissertation on how anthropomorphic climate change had affected plant physiologies in tundra latitudes, and a virtual ban from employment in major universities whose hiring decisions were channeled through IMC corporate donors who tasted an unsavory flavoring in her conclusions. WWP had slept late while IMC had gathered in the sheaves needed to control the science that would be discovered, how it would be discovered, by whom it would be discovered, and taught, by academicians regarding our changing physical world. But science was part of Melibea's DNA. She was not and could not be devoted to the liberal arts at a professional level. So she took what she expected to be a different, safely apolitical tack a few years ago—outer space. What could be less of a political study than that which was occurring (or more accurately had long ago occurred) hundreds, thousands, millions, billions of light years away from Mother Earth? No money to be made out there. What politician or corporate bigwig could fret over, or hold against her, facts she might discover in the galaxies beyond? The sibilant "s" read on:

Naming rights for the two major American parties are awarded every four years for the following presidential election cycle. Minor parties still do not sell naming rights, claiming that doing so amounts to a slap in the face of our democratic system. Others contend that the minor parties would suffer embarrassment when bidders and bids would be disappointing or non-existent. . . . .

But time for Mel was running out. Just less than a year ago she had excitedly delivered her programmed sequence of movements that Henrietta's operators were to provide her to view Melibea's target area. Then, with the use of Henrietta's advanced fine guidance sensors and the help of the tracking and data relay satellite system, Henrietta's controllers had returned what she had asked for in abundance. Mel, and a handful of her fellow scholars associated with her project team, had been peering at an area that had held her interest, but thereafter she had had to discard one and another and another false lead. After a few weeks more, Henrietta's beautiful little album of the stars would be released to the public, and evidence of any supernova she might have overlooked, or not had time enough to even view at all, would be her baby stolen from the warming table next to her delivery bed before Mel could even once hold the infant next to her. She must keep looking, and looking assiduously.

Melibea's target area was nestled in an elliptical galaxy in the southern constellation of Hydrus, and indexed as PGC6240, commonly known as The White Rose Galaxy. It was the elegant shape of PGC6240 which made inspiration for its nickname apt and for humans almost inevitable. The older Hubble telescope's enhanced image of The White Rose Galaxy closely resembled a small flowering plant which grows on a tiny faraway planet in a galaxy more than 340 million light years away, where it had been admired by generations of the dominant life form. And, for all the astronomical reasons, the floral appearance of The White Rose Galaxy made her selection not only one astronomically based but, for a botanist, the work of a moment.

Real estate sales in southern Alaska and northwest British Columbia have become so vigorous that property experts are calling that region the new northern California. Climate change has pushed warmer temperatures so far north buyers are flocking to the Ketchikan/Juneau areas, scooping up property while it is still relatively affordable.

In international news, the middle ea-----"

Mel switched off the radio. She hadn't been really listening to the news. The headlines were only a brief interruption between the classical music selections that were broadcast on her favorite station. That the classics appealed to her as they did she attributed to her finding that the form, arrangements, and composition of the classics supremely compatible with the movements of the stars and galaxies. Maybe she should give the Humanities more credit than she had previously.

With the radio now off, the silence in the room stirred Melibea to acknowledge that sitting and staring at a computer screen full of spectrographic observations for as long as she had was beginning to numb her mind, and glaze her eyes, and a check of the wall clock told her it was past midnight. Mel was not anti-social, but she preferred to work late at night when she could toil most proficiently, that is, without human distraction. Such distraction was most frequently provided by Ernst Tippleskirchen, a fellow *astra* grad assistant at the university. Ernst, or "Tip," was a nice enough chap, brilliant as well, and he was no masher. He was just a young man whose idea of multi-tasking was doing thing "A" while simultaneously chatting up anyone and everyone who happened to be within earshot. That was his undisputable talent, not Mel's. Most commendable was his charitable willingness to contribute both ends of the conversation whenever his would-be interlocutor turned decidedly reticent, supplying responses he thought the other would likely give if she were inclined to respond at all. Late at night, however, Tip found more fertile ground for reciprocal loquacity, alcohol induced, at *The Woebegone Wobbegong*, his and his boon companions', and most of the student body's, favorite beverage and live entertainment establishment.

But now it was beddy-bye time; time to say goodnight to Henrietta's picture show, quit peeping at the twinklies, close The Rose, log off the Astronomy Department's computers, and go home. Maxim, her "Max," would probably be sound asleep in their little bed in their little rooms in their little efficiency apartment. He was the early bird; she the night owl. And Max did have that big job interview tomorrow at Guardian Enterprises, LLC. He had said the work was something to do with Guardian Enterprises' Government Adjunct Department, whatever that was. Having been politically sabotaged and sensitized some years back, she thought it sounded vaguely ominous, but she would surely be told about it tomorrow. She wasn't certain of the veracity of the comment, but she had heard someone in the Department say in passing that GE, LLC was IMC owned. She hoped not.

CHAPTER 2

Maxim Markhov was pedaling his restored second-hand Schwinn 10-speed bicycle up the winding mile long asphalt entrance road to the gated office building of Guardian Enterprises, LLC, just before nine-o'-clock the next morning. He had gently kissed a sleeping Melibea before sliding out of bed around seven-thirty, quietly performing his ablutions, dressing, and noiselessly closing the apartment door behind him.

Dense rows of alder, white spruce and douglas fir grew with contrived human assistance over an unbroken groundcover of forsythia, azalea, rhododendron and other random artificially sustained flora on both sides of the entrance road. He had already been admitted past the first security gate bordering state highway 13 by a gaunt, pointy-nosed fiftiesh-looking guard whose shirt drooped loosely from his spindly shoulder blades, and trousers countered gravity only with the aid of a belt tightened enough to leave a full 10 inches of excess leather dangling from the last belt loop. The guard inspected Max and his Invitation to Interview letter from GE's human resources department with an eye that seemed to be courting some reason to refuse. The first entrance point was entirely unmarked; no sign, no lights, only the guard post. Had Max's Invitation to Interview, which had been hand-delivered by a runner for GE, not provided directions, he would have been unable to find the place. After a silent minute, Max's interpretation of a reluctantly given nod by his reviewer as a positive sign was confirmed by a buzzing sound and the raising of an automated turnpike which action told Max more than the human scarecrow had seen fit to say. He pedaled on.

As he approached to within 50 yards or so of the second entrance to the building, Max saw all trees and undergrowth abruptly and completely cease around the entire perimeter of the building and its keep, and the presence of a tall metal fence topped with razor wire above and bordered by concertina wire at ground level. Max braked before the second guard house, which was occupied by a man and woman, each bigger and beefier than the emaciated figure a half-mile back. Max was a muscular 28-year-old, above middle height, but these two were intimidating him. The impression was fortified by the side arms and assault rifles they were carrying.

"Maybe on my way out I'll tell Skinny Joe where he can find the people who are stealing his lunch every day," Max spoke *sotto voce* as he neared the male guard who already had a ham hand reaching out to him in a gesture unmistakably demanding papers, while the female guard stood in the middle of the road with both hands, palms out toward Max, reminding him of *Attack of the 50 Foot Woman.*

Max deftly reached into his shirt pocket and produced for the male guard the Invitation to Interview letter. As he perused it, Max smiled on female guard. Female guard frowned on Max. He removed his insulting eyes from the uniformed harridan to see male guard scan the computer bar code at the bottom of the letter across a small box just inside the door of the guard house. The box produced a small green light and a beep. Male guard returned the Invitation to Interview to Max. Max smiled on male guard. Male guard frowned on Max. The electronic metal gate silently opened, and female guard gave way, and shot her right arm outward in the direction of the opening, directing Max to enter into the keep, more as an order than an invitation. Max pedaled on, keeping his remaining smiles to himself.

"WELCOME TO GUARDIAN ENTERPRISES--

OUR PROTECTION SECURES YOU"

The sign some 20 feet above ground level was forged in steel with letters as tall as Max himself. It spanned above the entire width of the entranceway and was arced into a crescent, secured on either side of the pavement with bolts screwed into concrete pinions. Max passed under the sign and pedaled toward the smoked plate glass doors to the 11-story building. He was in.

Max locked his Schwinn to a mature larch next to the steps, and entered GE, LLC. At the security check point he emptied his pockets, kicked off his shoes, and stepped through the revealing full-body scanner. Max was no exhibitionist, but he did feel a slight boost of confidence, and flow of energy after all the hours spent in the gym. The scanner attendant, a not unattractive woman near Max's age gave Max his very first GE smile, albeit vicariously, not flattering Max, but his electronically reproduced full body image.

Found acceptable and made secure, Max strode over to the information booth and was greeted by a second more toothsome smile in the mouth of a large, professionally attired, woman of middle age, whose clothing exuded a fruity aroma of a scent profligately applied by its owner some hours since. Her ample hair was wound atop her head with every strand partnered with its mates, and held completely motionless by what could have been furniture lacquer.

"May I help direct you, sir?" she offered, and before waiting to hear if Max needed any help, stated what she thought really important. "I'll need to see your Guardian Enterprises invitation letter." Another demanding hand extended to Max. He again produced, what was becoming a rather crumpled, spindled, Invitation to Interview letter, which she eagerly took from him. Her smile's utility expended, it disappeared. She scanned the letter's bar code into another little box and waited with her red lipsticked lips pushed out, reserving the teeth to allure the next visitor's papers, and watched for information to appear on her computer screen.

"You must see Mr. Amberguese, in Government Adjunct. I'll inform him that you're in the building, Mr. Markhov," she said to Max and into her telephone with the seriousness of a physician announcing a patient's diagnosis of pathology. "Thank you," Max said to her concretized hair.

The summons completed, Max was directed to seat himself in the lobby area, and wait for Mr. Amberguese. The information woman inquired if Max would like a bottle of water in a tone indicating mere mild curiosity into Max's state of hydration more than a willingness to bring him such refreshment were he to say yes. He said "No thanks."

Max slowly paced around the ornately tiled reception area, complete with several intricate, circular tile medallions laid into the floor, the largest of which was every bit of 20 feet in diameter and depicted the ambiguous GE, LLC logo, showing in silhouette an avian raptor swooping down to either protect, scoop up, or devour, a human. Looking upward, Max saw that the entire 11 stories were open to the sunlit solar roof, with offices rising only on all four sides of the square building, providing every office a view outward. Four centrally located elevators rose and lowered inside shafts rising all the way to the top floor, and at each floor a walkway extending out from the elevator doors set at 90 degree angles, to all four directions leading to the wall offices.

Verdant philodendron and arrowhead vines bearing deep green foliage cascaded down from the open interior catwalk around the four sides of one floor to the next lower floor, forming a nearly continuous interior of greenery from 11th to ground floor level. Around the floor were innumerable banana trees, fica trees, and other plants in pots large enough to accommodate a human. "It's a jungle in here," would be an expression approaching closer to literal than figurative speech.

"Excuse me, but are you Mr. Markhov? I'm Algernon Amberguese." Max wheeled about to see a corpulent figure held together by a three-piece suit, complete with boutonniere, necktie in red paisley with matching handkerchief adroitly placed in the suit coat pocket so as to leave enough material to only slightly drape over the pocket top. "Yes, please call me Max," Max offered his warmest handshake and smile.

"Algie," Algie said, returning a plump hand for shaking that he had just dried with a white handkerchief he kept stuffed up his right suit coat sleeve.

"Won't you please come with me? We in Government Adjunct are happy to know you." Max fell into step with Algernon—"Algie" might require some getting used to-- as they moved toward the block of elevators.

CHAPTER 3

"Here at GE's GA Department we work hard to provide GE's elected officials, our cooperating officeholders so to speak, with the high quality legislation and direction they need to insure the continued prosperity of America by furtherance of International Moderators Corporation's goals and those of its subsidiary companies, including Guardian Enterprises. We take no small pride in knowing that our members of congress and the legislature rarely need to lift a finger to do their jobs. We do virtually all of the heavy lifting within these walls. With our assistance they are freed to do what they do best and enjoy most—giving speeches, meeting with their voters, being part of media appearances, and spending more time with their families. In return, they relate back to us on the inclinations and prospects of our government members and their impending actions, keeping us informed on how better to mold their wills to improve the lot of all—something we work very hard to do."

Phyllis Winders was the Director of the Government Adjunct Department. She was tall, six feet easily, and a slim, angular, beautiful, cinnamon complected Black woman. She saw with languid hazel eyes which rested large in their orbits below a medium-length hairdo, curled with minimal layering, all components of an attractive head of natural salt-and-pepper hair. Her solid royal blue dress with scalloped half sleeves was tied at the waist, with pleats below waist. She displayed jeweled accessories which were impeccable in fit, color, and design. A pair of navy blue pumps with medium heels (she was only slightly self-conscious of her exalted altitude) completed her ensemble. Her movements were slow and deliberate. Her relaxed manner of speech could be deceiving only for the first minutes upon meeting her. Soon they would be found out to be only the result of utmost confidence in the rectitude and irrefutability of whatever she was saying. Her words defied dissent, and were spoken by a sure woman who had seldom experienced any such repugnant challenges.

"We find ours a mission you might find compatible with your communication aptitudes, Max, and hope you have drawn a similar conclusion. Have you?" Winders asked, with her casual voice and eyes cast at Max, accompanied by an expectation of nothing other than his unequivocal, affirmative response.

"Absolutely," was all Max could muster in the moment, looking at Winders's forehead, fearing his hypnosis if he were to continue making direct eye contact with this person.

Algernon slightly clinked his teacup on its saucer as if signaling his request to contribute an additional comment. The small noise attracted the other eyes in the room, and he grabbed at the opportunity.

"I would only add to what Phyllis said that the GA Department, in addition to writing the very bills which frequently, but never often enough to suit us, become passed into law, also goes the extra mile by providing guidance to our cooperating officeholders even in the area of their public utterances and publications. They are always grateful for the assistance we provide them by way of communications that will cause not the slightest conflict or embarrassment due to misconstruction by the public or the unsecured media outlets. We never want our cooperating officeholders to be at odds with IMC or GE sentiments and purpose, and neither do they. Our relationships are ones of mutual trust and reliance." Algie was holding teacup and saucer in his left hand, aided by the assistance of his midriff amply extended by a seating position. His white handkerchief was now poised at the ready on his right knee in preparation of his hands again exuding excessive liquid.

"Quite." Winders relieved Algernon Amberguese with one word that told him that his remarks had not been an offense against the nobility of GE's mission to channel its government into a positive direction. "So then, Max," Winders began, as she placed her cup and saucer on the small table next to her chair, uncrossed her legs, and stood up, *way* up, "if you have no more questions," beaming a smile, extending a hand, "I'll be the first to welcome you as our newest congregant." Max popped up and crossed the short distance to Winders.

"Thank you, Ms. Winders," handshake between them, followed by five unobtrusive, brief and slightly moist handclaps from Amberguese.

"If you'll go with Algie now he will show you around our little facility, and you can begin in-processing here tomorrow morning at eight-o'-clock. Better then; tomorrow commences a new pay period. Algie make sure Max is bar coded to enter tomorrow. Max, you'll receive your permanent picture ID and be coded as part of in-processing tomorrow. Have the nicest day." Winders strode out of the room, the paradigm of Woman with Purpose, leaving Algie and Max momentarily frozen in their place.

Passage of another 30 or 40 minutes had seen Algie give Max his paper printed with the bar coded entrance pass dated for tomorrow, their tour of the facility and grounds of the keep, and by then they were strolling back to the front doors of the office building. As they approached the entranceway gate, Max briefly thought it odd that the huge overarcing "WELCOME" sign was coldly blank on its opposite side, a brooding silence to all who had come and were now departing.

Suddenly, the first bars of Rimsky-Korsokoff's *Flight of the Bumblebee* began to emanate from somewhere inside Algernon Amberguese. "Oh, you will pardon me please Max while I tend to this call." Algie excavated a videophone from the depths of his inside suit coat pocket. "It's one of our cooperating officeholders."

"Sure. No worries." Max halted and Algernon padded over a few steps to a park bench beneath the shade of a large birch tree to answer the call. He laid his burden down on the bench, and with a voice that carries at what for Algie was a normal pitch, began speaking to a member of congress, audible to Max.

"Hello Carl. All is well with you and yours?"

. . . .

"Hadn't we thought that was going to be shot down in the Senate today."

. . . .

"They did?

. . . .

That many?

. . . .

"Uh-huh…I see."

. . . .

"Well what exactly came to light?"

. . . .

"But that isn't what they said in committee."

. . . .

"Uh-huh. I see. . . . But I don't find all of that as an insoluble problem, Carl. . . . Keep your feet on the ground, Carl. Those facts can be easily opinionized."

. . . .

"We'll put a team on it today. You just said that the House hearing's not scheduled until next Tuesday, and we can have you the material you need in 48 hours."

. . . .

"No need to thank me, Carl. Securing you is our job."

Algernon rang off and his congenial smile was erased only for a few seconds, and his countenance revealed an honest, thoughtful concern and even perhaps, Max thought, worry.

"Right, Max," the affable grin returning, "I must see you to the gate now. Duty calls. Not a large difficulty though. Just some small matter that's become unsecure, and flapping around in the political breeze. Not at all what our member needs. Must tie it down again, and all that, you understand I'm sure."

"Sure. I understand. Thank you for the tour." Algie accompanied Max for another furlong to near the gate, smiling his smile only intermittently now. When he stopped, he wiped his hand and shook Max's. Max continued on and walked through the gate that had opened so Guardian Enterprises, LLC could disgorge him until tomorrow. As he glanced back into the keep, he could see poor Algie making his way back into the building, handkerchief in hand, giving his exposed areas a full and thorough wipe down.

CHAPTER 4

By the time Max threw open the apartment door it was nearly noon, and Mel was standing at the kitchenette spreading some raw honey over her dry toast, and alternately sipping *café con leche* and juice.

"I got the job! You're looking at the newest employee of Guardian Enterprises, LLC. I start tomorrow!" He danced around the efficiency apartment like Fred Astaire, his incarnation of Ginger Rogers a brown-bagged bottle of red wine. Mel felt her love and happiness for Max surge within her. Perhaps she never loved him more than when she could see him in his boyish exuberance and delight, like a pre-adolescent who had just won the soap box derby, or hit a home run in a Little League game.

"Max that's wonderful! I'm so happy for you." Melibea instantly gushed excessive enthusiasm. She was indeed happy for Max and his achievement, but, well, concerned. Guardian Enterprises was still as unknown to her as parts of The White Rose Galaxy. "Let's celebrate with some breakfast-- or lunch, or brunch, or whatever the case may be."

"And we'll wash it down with some of this," he said unbagging and raising the dancing bottle.

"Well, tell me all about it. What's my man going to be doing in the coming days? Government work of some sort isn't it?" She smeared the honey over a slice of toast and took a bite.

"Yes, of some sort. I'll find out more exactly tomorrow, my first official day," Max said happily as he twisted open the bottle of wine. "But essentially they were impressed enough with my academic credentials in Speech and Communications to offer me a job in their Government Adjunct Department's Public Policy Support Unit. They work at giving direction to what they call cooperating officeholders." He reached into the tiny cabinet for two plastic cups and poured.

"Wow! Is your salary commensurate with the title? Hope so." Mel took a sip of café.

"Let me just say it will be enough for us to move out of this Cumberland Lakes kommunalka into a real apartment, maybe a two bed-room unit. Of course, once you start making the big bucks as a stargazer we might have enough to make a down payment on a house. Oh, not imme-diately, but maybe in a year or two. Mel, I'm so happy. Now we can do so much more together." Max moved over to the sofa with his cup of red, and sprawled out, the conquering hero.

Mel picked up her small plate of honeyed toast, and cup of juice, leaving behind for the nonce Max's offering of wine, and joined him on the other end of the sofa. She placed her plate on the small coffee table in front, holding her juice. "So this will be Monday through Friday, 9 to 5?"

Max swallowed a gulp of red and said "Far as I know. But they said sometimes political necessities call for us to work odd hours, you know, when the public really needs to be told what is real, when the other side is telling them something else. Well, Algie didn't put it exactly like that, but that's not the way he talks."

"Algie?"

"Algernon Amberguese—I'm not making that up. He's the Public Policy Support Unit Supervisor. He'll be my direct supervisor. Big guy, flashy dresser, booming voice, a few years older than you, but not much, maybe 40."

"Thanks. I think." Mel leaned forward toward the coffee table, positioning her face obliquely to Max's under cover of reaching for the second piece of toast. "And who might be 'the other side?'"

"Oh that's usually the WWP Democrats, but not always. That's World Wide Producers, Inc.—didn't think I knew that, did you? That's the main corporation that regulates the Democrats. But sometimes it's just groups or individuals giving the public, the voters, information that makes passage of laws favorable to IMC more difficult. That's when we come in. We prepare packages of our own information for our cooperating officeholders to disseminate—like that word?—it's Algie's"

Mel stood up to take her plate and café cup back to the kitchenette. "And what if the World Wide Producers Dems—or other groups or individuals—are telling the truth about something GE thinks makes it difficult?"

"Well, uh, Algie didn't really go into that. Main thing seems to be that we make sure it's easier for the cooperating officeholders to pass the laws GE writes. . . . I'm sure they're good laws."

Here Mel looked ahead and saw the hitherto smooth conversational path starting to become more treacherous. She wanted to choose her next question carefully, or maybe not ask a next question at all. She decided to risk one more throw.

"Oh, by the way, speaking of the WWP Democrats, did you find out for sure if GE is owned by IMC?" She braced.

"Melibea," he began. Mel had learned that Max's usage of *Melibea* in lieu of *Mel* was his Serious Signal to her. She dialed up her mansplaining receptors in anticipation of the receipt of some ill-considered, blunt declarations and interrogatories for the next few minutes.

"I know what happened to your Botany career, and I know you said that was directly because of IMC, and I'm sorry. But these aren't the same people who hurt you. Wish you could have met them today. They're all very nice, and just want their officeholders to be able to pass laws that are helpful."

"Helpful for GE?"

"GE does a lot of good."

"Good for GE? For IMC?"

"Damn it, Melibea, I finally have a start to a career, and all you seem to take pleasure in is criticizing me and those who are giving me, giving us, a chance." Max stood up and walked away to the window overlooking Cumberland Lakes' grassy front lawn with two little ponds that had been dug to about six feet of depth, lined with plastic, at regular intervals filled by water trucks, edged with quarried four-inch rock, landscaped with a few cattail, and artificially sustained.

"No I don't Max. I really don't." She started to slowly approach him to offer a conciliatory overture. "It's just that, well, don't you *ever* think about the social implications and impacts of your actions?" Max wheeled about expressing anger and disappointment in his face.

"And don't you *ever* think about anything *else*?!" He stalked to the apartment door and down the stairs and out the front door of the apartment unit. Mel looked out the window and saw him pedaling away on his Schwinn.

CHAPTER 5

Melibea absentmindedly turned the pages of her astronomical journal borrowed from the university, the photos and words barely making an imprint on her mind. Hours after the fact, her thoughts were still reverberating, roiling in the mood of emotional discomfort brought on by the argument with Max. Those thoughts effectively blocked out any others as they would begin to enter. Mel was disappointed more than she was angry or upset. She had no animosity for Max. She reproached herself for going one question too far. Max was only doing what he needed to do. She just wished she had waited and let the information about Guardian Enterprises' work come to her instead of pressing for it. There had been no hurry. She would find out all in the fullness of time. And maybe it wouldn't be so bad.

Perhaps they would have him working on the peripheries where his hands could stay clean, she continued to imagine, *or at least not become indelibly stained.*

If he were going to work for those IMC bastards, it was not for her to interfere. His life, not hers. My God, she thought, *did I just think that? Hadn't our lives become intertwined? Why did I just now think of them as being separate?*

Max had pedaled out five miles to a city-county park sprawling across more than 500 acres, and kept lush with the artificial support systems of humans who could visit the park and be almost convinced by the outward fecundity that nature's self-sustaining cycles were still a given. He pedaled around the perimeter bike path several times, brooding, avoiding other cyclists and pedestrians, but sometimes not by much. He thought it better to pull over next to the most inviting shady spot, and do his brooding beside a tree.

Once there, he sat leaning against a sycamore, and his thoughts organized themselves better. *Why was Mel so damned concerned about what corporations and government did? Isn't a paycheck the main consideration? He knew how she felt about IMC and the IMC Republican Party, but he had no inkling or interest about any of that. IMC Republicans or WWP Democrats, what difference? If there were any, he didn't know what they could be. She was always carping about how the WWP Dems wanted to help people, but isn't that what GE did?. . . . . . His mind then searched but found no answer to that question. Did GE help people? Algie and some others had told him as much that morning, but. . . . . was Mel right? What was he getting into?*

The shadows were long and the sun lowering on the horizon, when Max stood up, and raised his bike. He pedaled slowly back to the Cumberland Lakes apartment complex, resolved that he would find out more about his new employer and what they did, how they did it.

Mel distractedly put a few plates and cups and flatware in the soapy dishwater, avoiding the opened, nearly full bottle of wine which looked to her like a beheaded casualty of war, left on the field of battle. Then she knew she needed to go somewhere. Go to the planetarium's computer room. Just to be with other astronomers and surrounded by science would be a comfort. She playfully smiled as she considered how ironic it would be if Tip should be there, and she could reverse their roles by trying to light up a gab fest with him while he worked. She threw on her parka, pushed into her running shoes, grabbed her tote bag, and was out the door.

CHAPTER 6

Pulling up to the bicycle racks outside the university's planetarium, Mel locked her old racing bike to the rack, shouldered her tote bag and started up the steps. The planetarium and adjoining offices of the Astronomy Department were originally constructed in the 1960s, but the original edifice had been remodeled and enlarged twice since. The planetarium itself was designed more for function than form. There were no architectural flourishes or flights of fancy constructed from the imagination of an inspired architect. The buildings were solid, red brick, square, with square windows. But the pride of the Astronomy Department was reserved not for packaging of the planetarium, but its contents. The university's planetarium boasted three telescopes; a 5.1-meter telescope, and a 2.1-meter telescope, each outfitted with the latest state-of-the-art optics and light gathering components; not the largest earth-bound telescopes, but not too shabby for a state institution of higher education. There was also a small 15-inch telescope that could be enjoyed by the public, amateur sky watchers, and school groups.

A group of bright-eyed undergrads from Melibea's Astronomy 101 class encountered her at the entry doors.

"Oh hi, Dr. Paz. How you?"

"Not going to be too rough on us with next week's quiz are you?" The two young women wearing backpacks and carrying videophones paused at the doors.

"Now I don't think I could possibly be so rough as to keep you guys from acing any quiz I might give. Just tell some of the others to study as much as you do, will you? Gotta run now."

"G'bye Doctor Paz."

Mel climbed the stairs to the large computer room and surveyed the situation. Sure enough, Tip was at his usual spot, and a couple of other astronomical acquaintances were at other computers, deeply engrossed in what she had no idea. She snuck up behind Tip, surprised again by the grin she already felt spontaneously spreading on her face as she approached his long, lean back with his wavy, light brown hair pouring down his neck.

"Hello Tip. Still plotting Cepheids in our very own Milky Way? Don't you ever want to leave our neighborhood and actually go somewhere? You really ought to take a vacation, get a few hundred light years away from it all."

Tip turned around and beamed at Mel. "Yep, still plotting Cepheids, but only for a little while. These are only peripherally related to my thesis, but I have to touch all the bases. Some others of your team were here for a couple of hours, just left. They didn't see anything. But don't lose heart Mel. I still think the most promising areas you targeted are the ones you haven't even seen yet."

"Thanks, Tip. No chance I'm giving up on my SN until I've reviewed every square inch of my search field, twice."

"You're here early for a night owl. Better be careful. Max will be getting jealous of your time spent here," Tip said, wagging his finger at her with intended humor. Mel's smile evaporated.

"Oh, Max doesn't know I'm here; and it wouldn't matter." She looked away, downcast.

Tip noticed. "Something seems to matter, and not in a good way. Care to talk about it? You know me, talk, talk, talk. And with friends-- that would include *you*, by the way-- I'll even tolerate tossing the verbal ball back and forth about something *ser-i-ous*, if you think it might help."

"Thanks, Tip, but no. It's just a thunderclap. It'll pass." Melibea tried to resurrect her dead smile, and failed miserably. "But I did feel a need to come here, and be with" she caught herself like a person who isn't watching where she's going and looks up just in time to avoid bumping into a hard truth, "my work. . . .and colleagues," she spilled a diluted reality. "My year is almost up you know, and after that my fate could be spending my dotage pointing to a supernova in an astronomical journal and boring any grand-kids I might still have a small chance to see with the story of how the image really should have Na-na's name under it."

"You'll find it, Mel. . . . But OK then. Offer still stands. Anytime. So, I have to leave now." He started cramming notebooks, handheld computers, and plotted variable sheets into his backpack. "I've been so occupied with my thesis that I neglected to prepare a little quiz for my 101 class. Sit down, and keep looking. Your SN is there." Tip sincerely suggested. He shoul-dered his backpack, and paused. "You know, it's been my experience that taking my brain light years away from life's little vexations, and hanging with the stars, never fails to chase the blues away."

"You're right. Time 'to boldly go where no one has gone before' and all that. Thanks for the bolstering Tip. I feel better already. I owe you one."

"I'll collect payment on that debt by way of that championship smile I see from you so often. Most people smile only with their mouth, but did you know that when you smile you smile with your whole face. It's like the full moon shining on me. It really is something to see." Tip was at the door.

"See ya Tip. You really are *El Chavo Fresa*, you know?"

"What am I?"

"I'll have to explain it later, maybe. It doesn't really translate well." Mel said, not wanting to translate it well. Tip grinned and pushed both hands through his long hair, front to back, smiled his own championship smile, and went away.

Mel wasted no time returning to the outer petal-like shell of The White Rose Galaxy that was by now her home away from home. Knowing her surfeit of optimism that ran rampant when the first spectrographic data was received had been abraded by looking and looking but never seeing more than what everyone already knew was in PGC6240, Mel mustered her last reserves of that limited and precious quantity of persistent confidence that enables a scientist to strive, to discover, to prove that we now know more than we did, sometimes much more, Mel raised her eyes to scan yet another image at one of the gossamer layers made of thousands of stars revolving far away from the center of The White Rose.

She checked herself when, upon seeing that next image, she opened in her mind a debate of how many of these starry rejection notices she could bear to look at this time, but then drew upon her remaining resolve to steel herself, and tell herself that this one, this one will be the oyster with the pearl.

And then, after meticulously viewing scores and scores of data pages, and every tiniest portion of enhanced images she had by that hour stopped counting, then. . . . there *was* something. Mel wasn't sure *what* it was, but it was something on the petal she had not seen for almost a year of her looking. She was almost incredulous. She wanted, and simultaneously did not dare, to believe her own eyes. It was like the mail carrier had just left at her doorstep a package she opened to find the loveliest object of art she had ever beheld, and her first reaction was to look at the mailing address to make sure it hadn't been misdelivered.

She looked dizzily away from the computer screen to look at anything else-- at astronomical posters on the wall, at the windows in the room and the darkness outside, at the floor. And then she looked back at the computer. And it was still there. There, on an area in the lower left hand side of the last image she could bear to look at that evening, she saw it. And she was transfixed, transfixed by looking at what appeared to be nothing but a small, even tiny, smudge.

CHAPTER 7

Mel's fingers began saving and printing back up of this beauty in every format and as quickly as she possibly could. The cup at her lips, she was not going to risk having it dashed from her hands before she could know the taste of its contents. And who to tell first, for she had to have someone else see this to make it really real. Then the laborious, meticulous process of actual confirmation of a supernova had to be endured. At every step of that way others would be doing their dead level best to disprove it, but that did not make them malicious, only scientists. That was the way of science she knew; not to hastily conclude in favor of what one wishes were so, and then refuse to consider other possible explanations. Nor was it science to pay charlatans who were paid by an interested and biased think tank to crank out scientific-sounding work. But it was to elevate the seeming to the real only after all other possible explanations have been fairly ruled out.

But for now her nervous joy needed a human outlet for expression. The room was now empty but for a few people casually studying in books or on computers. Not they. Tip was long gone. Dr. Banks, the Chair of the Department of Astronomy and Astrophysics was in Paris attending a meeting of the *Académie*, not scheduled to return for two more days, and probably still asleep at this hour Paris time. Max! She could tell Max! She pulled her videophone out of her tote, and turned it on, and just as she was pressing the apartment phone number cloud cover obliterated the whole idea. Maybe not Max; maybe not now. She had just stomped all over his first major career victory, or so he thought, which was all that mattered to the present purpose. How could she now parade before him her possible international astronomical discovery? She eased the phone back into her tote. There were others she could tell, and would love to share with eventually, but not now. No, the first choice obviously would have been Dr. Banks, who was largely responsible not only for Henrietta's being, but for Mel heading up the team, and being given the honor of choosing the target area, and nurturing her through this whole grueling but exciting process. But after her, who? Tip, who had contributed to the search and supported her as well, and actually been a member of the search team. Or Max?

She would not decide until she withdrew her videohone again and using her thumb scrolled down her speed dialing list. MAX: #417-6235, TIP: #312-5683. . . . TIP. . . . MAX. . . . TIP . . . . MAX. . . .

She dialed, meekly applying barely enough pressure to her phone to make it work. . . .

"Hey you, whatever you're doing, drop it and come over to the planetarium, *now* ! There's something you have to see."

"Do tell," Tip's voice replied amid the ambient background noise of people conversing, and recorded music playing.

"I see a little smudge on my screen." Mel's breath was coming in short gasps.

"There's a brand new box of screen wipes right behind the computer I was using earlier today."

Mel laughed. She could laugh now seeing Tip on the videophone; it felt good. "No, you ninny. You know what I mean. This could be it; this could be something. Come on over. I need to share this with someone."

"I just walked into the *Wobb*. It'll take me about 20 minutes." Tip rang off and walked out the door of *The Woebegone Wobbegong*, abandoning a freshly poured draft on his table to be adopted by his companions.

CHAPTER 8

Once the initial ecstasy of the realization subsided, which included chasing each other around the halls of the planetarium and not caring about the puzzled looks from its other inmates, Mel and Tip for the next two days poured over every item, every spectrograph they could in the short time before Dr. Banks returned from Paris. They had to take this to her; let her coordinate the verification process between Mel and her search team, and Henrietta's ground crew, with special emphasis on her X-ray telescopic findings. They had to find out as soon as possible if this were an actual early stage supernova, showing itself before peak brightness, and if so of which variety. Will the new data reveal the presence or absence of any hydrogen signature in the light spectra as in a Type 2 or Type 1, presence of silicon in the spectra as in a Type 1a, or the signature of helium as in a Type 1b, or neither silicon nor helium as in a Type 1c. Or a mini-supernova, a 1ax. The questions rushed through Melibea's head almost too fast to be absorbed by her thoughts. Time, so much time would be needed to answer those questions, or so it seemed to Mel who had suddenly become as impatient as a three-year-old. Meanwhile, Mel had to take what she had so far and put it before Dr. T. A. Banks, who would soon return from Paris.

Doctor Trailing Arbutus Banks was named after the wildflower that used to grow abundantly in the Appalachian Mountains. Her students called her "Doc T.A." Her friends and peers called her "Trail" or Dr. Banks. She was petite, and would be barely 5'2" in heels, but she would never wear heels, preferring comfortable sandals or pair of slippers cleverly disguised as shoes. She weighed all of 105 pounds, and it was often said that 100 pounds of that was brains. Dr. Banks had looked through her first telescope when she was but ten years old, and had been with the university over 40 years, back to her matriculating there as an incoming freshman. She followed the same course Mel was now pursuing, and with every step of the way, increased her and the university's standing in the world of Astronomical academia. Her post-doctoral work was stellar, which is a pun and not a pun at the same time. Although her name was virtually unknown outside academia, inside her orbit it would be impossible to step inside an astronomy office or department anywhere and not be able to lay hands on any number of publications authored entirely by her or including published articles referencing the esteemed Dr. T. A. Banks. She had been Chair of the University's Department of Astronomy and Astrophysics for more than 15 years. She had been twice offered a Deanship, and twice refused out of an abiding love for her present position.

Mel and Tip were waiting in the reception area adjacent to Dr. Banks's office, the former fidgeting, and the latter chatting up the office receptionist with degrees of success fluctuating like the various light curves on his Cepheid plots. At length, a door opened and the diminutive Dr. Banks emerged, smiling, as chipper as ever, showing no signs of any jet lag.

"Hello Melibea, Ernst. Please do come in. Bring me up to date on what was happening long ago," Dr. Banks quipped as she invited her visitors standing at the threshold with a graceful sweep of her arm.

Dr. Banks escorted them into her office and after stepping onto a flat wooden box placed behind her desk, seated herself on a thick cushion resting on an antique hickory fanback chair, thereby boosting her to a level sufficiently comfortable for desk work. It was either that or saw off the legs of the desk, which was also an antique of the same provenance as the chair, being the only two remaining articles salvaged from the fire that had consumed her grandparents' home in Gaffney, South Carolina. After exchanging pleasantries, chit-chat about Paris and the *Académie internationale de physique et d'astronomie*, for which Dr. Banks served as a member of the board, Mel spread out data sheets and images on a table across the room, and the trio began pouring over all, asking and sometimes answering questions, oftentimes reserving judgment as premature. Dr. Banks's frequent comment was a thoughtful "Umm-hmm, uhh-huhh."

Dr. Banks removed and folded her reading spectacles, placed them in their case and the case in the pocket of her print cotton blouse.

"Well," she commenced to pronounce, "of course we need further verification from Henrietta after we have directed her to provide more imagery and spectrographic data, zeroing in on Mel's smudge in PGC6240, naturally so we can see any signatures of helium, hydrogen, silicon, or their absence. And, of course we will ask if she can verify the smudge as a high density binary. Melibea, you and Ernst work up the sequence of movements to be programmed so Henrietta can be turned back again to the correct direction, and I will then use what juice I have to cut in line so we can receive confirmation, or not, from Henrietta. I will also contact my Chilean friend Miqueas at Cerro Tololo, and sweet talk him. Perhaps he will look and see if he can detect something for us from the southern hemisphere." She shrugged as if to say what will be will be, and walked across the table to stand directly facing Mel. "But," she reached out and grasped both of Mel's hands into hers, "based on Melibea's educated guess, as well as mine, that binary systems are present in this area, and the smudge itself, I would not be surprised if we find the further, more specific spectrographic and x-ray data to show some variety of a SN1 beginning to throw a cosmic temper tantrum." Her eyes were twinkling, and then Mel's began to tear, and Tip's fists shot high above his upraised head, and hugs, hugs, hugs went all round.

CHAPTER 9

The days and days of waiting for confirmation were excruciating for Mel, made no more bearable by the unease that still pervaded the little efficiency in the Cumberland Lakes Apartment complex. Henrietta was not exclusively dedicated to her astronomical search, however nice a fantasy that might be. Max had been learning the ropes with Guardian Enterprises, and was not sulking and moping about the place, or even being difficult as a house mate. But there was something changed about him, not for better or worse. He sometimes seemed to be preoccupied, lost in his thoughts about some subject or subjects far away from Mel. That circumstance itself was not at all Maximian. His unshakable insouciance about all of life's deeper questions, and impatience only with those who would try to make him take seriously anything beyond a roof that doesn't leak and food on the table was his personality. So his displays of introspective silence did not seem to consist with anything he had said about his work at the GE fortress, as they had come to call it. From all his short responses to her light touches upon the subject, she had gathered that he and Mr. Amberguese had started off on the right foot together, and he was a contributing member of his Unit, doing well in all regards. Mel and Max were superficially back to normal in nearly all respects, between and out of the sheets, after quarreling over the nature of the soul of IMC, or if IMC had a soul, and the implications on the soul of those who worked for that global control freak. So what was it? She couldn't lay her finger on it.

They had had an hour together early morning. Mel had risen earlier than her normal time to be with him. He was always at his best early morning, just after his long hot shower and coffee. Then were the times she could more safely but gingerly approach certain delicate subjects. He had been as of late expressing decided neutrality about the work he was doing, devoid of the enthusiasm he had hitherto unquestioningly exhibited. Then one morning, while Henrietta's anticipated findings were due at any time, Mel was relaxing on the sofa, eyes closed, communing with Mendelssohn, when Max raised one ear bud away from her to say good-bye.

"I have to leave for the fortress now, Mel." She removed both buds and sat upright. "Algie has a new project he's presenting to the Unit today. He gave me a little preview of it yesterday in the elevator. Wants me to find out what I can about some hayseed newspaper columnist whose throwing his weight around, writing naughty things about one of our—I mean GE's, not my—state cooperating officeholders. Our Unit is going to start working to opinionize his facts. My part seems to be finding evidence to discredit the source. Others in the team are creating a counterfactual narrative, and we will finish with a monograph we'll give our co-op offs." Max paused, leaving a conversational opening, but Mel demurred. Max leaned over the sofa back and instinctively Mel turned her head and returned his good-bye kiss. She touched his clean shaven face and smiled.

"Be home your usual time?

"Don't see what would keep me."

"Salad and fish sticks OK? If I'm not here when you come home, I'll leave them in the warmer for you. Not the salad; the fish sticks."

Max laughed. "Sounds good. See ya." He was out the door. Mel resumed listening to *Songs Without Words*, Felix's and Max's. Max was figuratively singing to her just then, but not with so many words. He seemed to be enjoying his work, but was trying to say without saying that he was keeping a professional distance. She was nearly asleep when her video-phone, setting on her tummy, began buzzing. She picked up.

"Hello."

"Hello, Melibea. Henrietta's answers are here. We also received an electronic data packet from Cerro Tololo. Miqueas is such a dear." Dr. Banks said. "We're waiting for our team leader to unveil what she saw. When can you be here?

"I'm as good as there now." Mel rang off and fairly levitated off the sofa.

CHAPTER 10

Algie led Max into a snack room and chose a table farthest away from the only other two employees in the room.

"Sit down Max. Coffee? Danish?" Algie stood at the serving counter, both arms reaching for plates and utensils to receive all his chosen savories.

"Just coffee, black. No Danish. Thanks." Max took a seat and Algie poured and delivered a cup of java to Max as a mere preliminary, and returned to the snack bar to collect his various and substantial comestibles. In a minute or two Algie returned and solemnly set down on the table with one hand a small plate groaning to accommodate a Danish, a Bear Claw, a bagel, and with the other hand sank four black teabags to the bottom of a 24-ounce cup of hot water.

"Max," he pulled up a chair, "I have recently concluded that something someone said about GE and IMC is bothering you. Something about the IMC Republicans and all those who help them being a walking, talking Mephistopheles. Am I close?" He bit off Bear Claw toes.

"Yeah, I mean I was just wondering what do you say to those people, maybe WWP Dems, when they say those things?"

"Max," Algie began as he wiped Bear Claw residue from his fingers, "the World Wide Producers Dems and the International Moderators Corporation Republicans and their political ancestry have been competing against each other under different names since before the founding of the republic. It ever was and ever shall be. It's an old and tiresome theme. Today, the dominant species in Washington, the species that thrives at the top of the food chain, everyone in the IMC and its subsidiaries, everyone in WWP and its subsidiaries, all know that it's not about what the Framers said or wrote, or the Declaration, or the sacred Constitution any longer, it's about corporations making as much money as possible while maintaining a patina of democracy and the wallpaper of words—government of the people, by the people and for the people—for the people to read and feel good about. Let me guess. This person who has put the bug in your ear, he or she has talked about the wicked ways of IMC and IMC Republicans, and how their policy positions are anti-social, bad for the poor and downtrodden, unfair, unjust, etc., etc.?"

"That's about it," Max said turning his coffee mug round and round on the table with thumb and index finger.

"Max, with a few pious exceptions, no one at IMC or at WWP for that matter, or anyone affiliated with them, least of all their cooperating officeholders, give a rat's tail about social issues, and the pious exceptions are free to be pious because they're still officeholders who cooperate with either IMC or WWP when it comes to the policies and votes that matter to IMC or WWP. Those boring culture wars are fought with some of the weapons we and the opposition manufacture for the sole motivation of equipping our respective co-op offs with a truth to compete against the other corporation's co-op offs' truth," Algie said, flourishing what remained of his Bear Claw around in the air. "But the officeholders owe and pay their fealty to the corporations, which they pay more obsequiously every year, not the people who only vote in an election staged to create the illusion of choice between values and priorities when the only choice is between competing corporate interests. The game being played by IMC and WWP is which of them is going to capture more cooperating officeholders. To capture more than the other means that one of us will see laws enacted that will make more money for us than the other guys. If one of the two ever captures a large enough majority of co-op offs it could drive the other into the ground, and win all the money. The reality though is that IMC and WWP have achieved and inescapably locked themselves into such a state of competitive equipoise that such an outcome will probably never happen. So the game will just go on forever, one side always trying to capture more officeholders so as to make it easier to make more money. All the while change in the social issues amounts to some of the laws and policies moving a little this way for a few years, and then moving a little back the other way for the next few years, and we. . . . don't. . . . care.

"Are you a WWP Dem, Max?" Algie pointedly asked, putting Max on the defensive.

Max hesitated for only a moment. "Yeah, I am. I mean I registered as a WWP Dem because Mel, I mean this person, wanted me to be a Dem. I don't get involved in politics though. Hope it's OK that I'm a Dem." Algie polished off the Bear Claw in this time, and was pushing the Danish on the plate with his fork, ready now to go in for the kill.

"Did anyone here ask you at your interview if you were a WWP Dem? No. Let me tell you something. You've met Jerry Snell in our Unit. Nice enough guy. Does good work. He's a WWP Dem. We don't care. Phyllis Winders herself is a WWP Dem. No one cares; least of all Jerry and Phyllis. You want to be a Dem, be a Dem; vote for WWP Democrats; we don't care. Max, some of IMC's co-op offs are WWP Dems, and some of WWP's co-op offs are IMC Republicans, not many, but some. We and WWP always have had a few strays, and sometimes some of them even switch allegiance, changing party affiliation. We pick off a few of the WWP's co-op offs and they occasionally pick off a few of ours. And we. . . . don't. . . . care. . . . about that either. The vote totals aren't substantially affected by them. But the strays or mavericks are strays only for votes IMC or WWP consider inconsequential, or votes when the whip count says the margin is safely in our favor or hopelessly lost anyway. The strays nearly always return to our fold for the close, important votes, the votes that touch and concern the corporate finances. Whenever those votes become prickly, we—and now you—will step in and create the facts and create the information, the weapons they need to neuter the criticisms, and maintain their own political health, which we then use to increase our corporate profits. We do as much for all our cooperating officeholders, because they haven't the ability, the time, the inclination, or the energy, to create these weapons themselves. They wanted a part-time job, and they have one. It imposes on their free time to have to spend every minute outside of congress grubbing for money, so IMC also serves to relieve them of that distasteful chore, by shoveling gobs of the wherewithal at their feet. And then, after we've done all that, even the strays who have not changed party affiliation vote for IMC, so the money spigot will not be turned off. And the same is true *vice versa* with the WWP and their officeholders. Once the cooperating members vote for IMC's or WWP's principles, *i.e.* money, they are free to go back and vote however what they call *their* principles, conscience, religion, values, whatever, tells them to vote for or against in the culture wars, votes which, as I said, neither IMC nor WWP cares about one iota. Their constituents think their member is God's own disciple, and the officeholder still cooperates within the fold, and the game goes on.

"Don't the officeholders have staff to do all the work we do?" Max ventured.

"Sure they have staff, staff to deal with constituent services, answer the phones, hand them *our* work in committee, and do the day-to-day humdrum of running an office. But IMC isn't going to yield our secured members we have diligently groomed and mentored to those outside our security wall, not when we are paying what we pay for an officeholder to cooperate. And who do you think employs most of what you call staff? Uncle Sam? He still pays the Senate pages. For most of the others, the ones that are process involved, we do, and we relieve the grateful taxpayers by picking up the tab for a chunk of the government's operating cost. Of course, our staff of our co-op offs who we pay are off-budget. We like it that way. Even so, the member of congress with our money shrinks his staff costs and look like a hero back home. More gratitude—and more important to us than gratitude, *obligation*-- flows to us.

"Our Government Adjunct Department has our Unit—yours and mine-- doing what I just reviewed, and our Legal Unit which actually writes the bills we need to see passed into law. We hand it all off to *our* staff of *our* cooperating officeholders, and we have an understanding about what they and we will do. What they do works for us, and what we do works for us, so everyone is happy."

"Now, I hope all of what I have said has allayed your apprehensions, Max. You will be comfortable here Max," Algie said with an inflection making it impossible for Max to discern if the last statement was an assurance, a question, or an order.

"I think I will be. Thanks, Algie."

"Splendid. Then let's get back to work." Max downed his now lukewarm coffee. Algie wrapped the surviving bagel in a napkin and pocketed the prisoner for later reckoning. They walked out of the snack room, back to work, back to creating weapons.

CHAPTER 11

Mel sat at the computer images, clicking on the next and the next. She was dumbfounded. Dr. Banks, Tip, and the other two team members standing behind her, looking over her shoulder were agog. What was that? Had Henrietta gone blind? Was there an error made by Mel, or by Cerro Tololo's ground crew? All of those were suggestions made by the team members, But Dr. Banks knew that none of that could be the problem causing what they saw. Most of the imagery on the wider screen images showed perfectly the area surrounding the targeted portion of PGC6240 containing the suspected early stage supernova. All the images showed the same; a perfect depiction of the galaxy right up to the edge of this black blob. But that area itself and what should have been closer, more detailed images of the suspected SN1 were, simply, gone. That area was blank, totally dark, completely deep-inside-a-cave black. And it was no tiny area, but a roughly circular expanse in the petal in The White Rose. Judging by the closer images, when the black area became progressively more of the entire image, it had to be approximately 10 or 11 parsecs wide.

Dr. Banks receded to a far corner of the room and was on her phone, speaking to colleagues in hushed tones for several minutes while Mel and the rest continued pouring over images of what made no sense. After some minutes she returned to the group, and the younger people looked to her for answers that she didn't have.

"I've spoken to my friends with Henrietta's ground team as well as my contacts at NASA and I was just on the phone with Miqueas. They are as intrigued as we are. Henrietta's people verified all programming was as we provided, and given to Henrietta accurately, and all equipment was functioning properly. No problems exist with the Tracking and Data Relay Satellite Systems. All of Henrietta's views of other regions in the universe are unremarkable for quality and content. No defects are present in the color enhancement, or other work performed by the Space Telescope Science Institute. But this is such a jarring phenomenon that Henrietta is going to be told to immediately start looking at the same area again. Of course that will take some time for her observations before we can have updated imagery and data outlining this. . . .opaque, black, globular area. Meanwhile, where we are now is: There is a hole in The White Rose Galaxy. We might say an entire petal seems to be lost"

"You mean a black hole, Doc. T.A?" the only undergraduate team member asked.

"No, no, not a black hole." What we are seeing is not at the center of PGC6240; it's at an outer edge, at one of what you sometimes hear called a petal of The White Rose. And none of the matter, stars, immediately adjacent to the—maybe I shouldn't call it a 'hole'—the void, seem to be affected to the slightest degree, let alone drawn into the void. And this void itself is an enormous area in size, and appears not to exert the slightest gravitational influence whatsoever. From what we can see so far, if we were in a spacecraft we could travel right up to the edge of the blackness without danger. Odd, very odd."

Then a smile overcame Trail's face and the youthful eyes twinkled again, "But science's mysteries are what attracted all of us to science in the first place, no?" She placed a reassuring hand on Mel's shoulder. "Melibea, we don't know what if anything happened to what you saw, but we all saw it. We know it was there, but now it's gone. Still, if spectacular astronomical discovery is what you longed to find, don't fret if what we thought was a SN1 is gone. If we can't find a mundane explanation for a galactic area approximately 35 light years across disappearing, then Melibea Paz will join others in the pantheon of history for finding, quite by accident and while looking for something entirely different, a phenomenon far more profound than any supernova. Does that not make you happy?" Mel responded with only a wan smile.

CHAPTER 12

"I can provide you today only a bare bones briefing on your weekly schedule assignments, as Phyllis has requested my presence at a one-thirty meeting with her and our lawyers from the Legal Unit, and I have lunch reservations for twelve," Algie gave excuses to members of the assembled Public Policy Support Unit in reverse order of importance.

"Ellacinda and Jerry: You're to work with co-op off and freshman state Sen. Wattkin Crottels beginning as of now. You may be aware of an organized effort to slightly reduce business property tax depreciation credits to help pay for more education. Such a reduction would adversely affect IMC corporations statewide, so-o-o-o-o, we must oppose it. Crottels is one of our low-tax co-op offs in the Senate."

"Aren't those credits already pretty generous in our state, Algie? Jerry Snell asked.

Algie gave Jerry the look of a parent regretfully searching for words to speak to a wayward child. "Yes. They are, Jerry. They're quite generous, thanks to GE, and I can say without fear of contradiction, thanks to me as well who worked to enact those quite generous credits some years ago when I was sitting in the chair you now occupy. And we mean to continue our government's generosity.

"Ellacinda, you and Jerry go to archives on the 5th floor. Archival records have numerous publications by IMC economists factualizing Sen. Crottel's values, opinions, utterances, and how repealing the credit and giving more money to education would hurt education. Pay special heed to those which factualize the rising success in numbers of home-schooled children, and the performance of the eager little ones who do so much better under the loving tutelage of their M&P, and so forth. WWP loves to play the Hurting Children Card against us, making that area a recurring vexation in our lives. So tread with caution, that aspect must be handled sensitive to perception. While you two are archive diving, I have instructed Crottels to simply stop talking in terms of opinion and simply maintain his position as proven, undisputable fact. There's so much material in archives that we can conjure up for him all the factualization he needs.

"Max: We need you to do some field work this week, and I do mean field work. Maybe I mentioned something of this to you a few days ago. Hitherto little known local farmer Pa Pat Paul Plymel has become known to us, and what is more of a problem, to many others, as a writer of letters and opinions in our local rag criticizing some of the beneficial chemicals IMC corporations brew up in their labs. He farms organically on a rather large tract about twenty miles from here. Here's his contact information." Algie tossed a small piece of a paper Max's way. "Need you to visit him, today if possible, and just flatter him-- say how you've read his pieces in the newspaper, interested in his position on the issue of chemicals on farms, and so forth. Photos of any sun baked crops, or dilapidation in his structures or equipment could be useful. If his aren't sun baked or dilapidated, same photos of his neighbor farmers' buildings or crops that are might be useful. Whatever you can produce to undermine or opinionize his facts. But don't antagonize the man; he's said to be highly irascible, and larger than I am. No confrontations. Last thing we want. Do this quietly.

"And be careful when you're out there as his is a family operation. There's your target: Pa Pat Paul Plymel, and his son Pat Paul Plymel, and the old man, Pappy Pat Paul Plymel, who usually stays indoors in front of the television. Make sure you know who you're talking to. Pa Pat Paul's wife is also out there."

"And her name is Paula, right?" Max created a laugh in the room.

"Don't know, don't care. She'd be a waste of your time. Sorry to send you on this one alone, Max. You were to have been paired with Ayesha, but she came down with some intestinal disorder. Must have been something she ate. The food she ate started making round trips. Pity. Never been a problem of mine. Food entering my alimentary canal is like a lost soul passing through Dante's Gates of Hell. 'Abandon All Hope, Ye Who Enter Here.'

"Any-questions-thought-not-you-guys-are-wonderful." Algie was out the door.

. . . .

Max found the Plymel farm without difficulty, spotting the name on the rural mailbox at roadside. The frontage of the Plymel place was bordered by a barbed wire fence, and an open dirt driveway ascending for some 100 yards to a large, antique wood frame farm house where large evergreens stood sentinel. An array of elderly vehicles in every stage of decay was parked off to the side of the house. Some Max thought might still move without being pushed or towed. Others had been left for dead long ago.

Max walked his bicycle up the dirt driveway which was deeply scarified, bearing the rutted wounds inflicted by years of tires and rain water runoff. Veritable gullies escorted the driveway up and down both sides. As Max walked up the driveway, handlebars in hand, he could hear the increasing volume of country and western music which seemed to be coming from behind the house, but the acoustics being what they were it was difficult for him to be sure. Max leaned his Schwinn against a tree trunk, and walked up the half dozen creaking, swayed front porch steps.

The windows facing the front porch were open preparatory to admitting a breeze into the house, should a breeze ever stir. The inside front door was open, and Max rapped gently a few times on its frame and waited. He heard and saw the flickering images of an old black-and-white movie playing on a television set, and heavy footfalls on the wood floors approaching from the deep recesses within. A woman's form began to appear and its features resolve in the dimness of the entrance. She was of middle-age, stern countenance of a woman whose prejudice was set against anyone who thought they needed to knock on her door. Those who enjoyed her welcome were those who didn't think it necessary to knock. Those who knocked probably shouldn't be at her house. She wore a short haircut of a dyed redhead, a western styled denim shirt, blue jeans, and cowgirl boots that had contributed to the floor-shaking Max had heard as she trod across the hall and living room. It was only her look at Max through the screen that asked "What do you want?"

"Excuse me, my name is Max Markhov and I was hoping to be able to speak with Mr. Pa Pat Paul Plymel for only a few minutes," Max asked as politely as anyone could.

"He's around back with Pat Paul," the formidable faux redhead said, beginning to feel relieved that this imposition would not be hers to bear but for a moment. "They're busy clipping the newborns' teeth, but your welcome to go around and see him," she gestured to her right, Max's left, with her whole body, and waited for Max to sidle off in that direction.

"Thank you very much." Max accommodated, walking down the porch steps which successfully bore human weight for at least one more trip. As Max found his way around to behind the house and approaching a barn and nearby pig sty, he wondered what kind of home dentistry this family practiced on its children, and if they birthed mutant children, born with teeth, or fangs, that required clipping. As he neared the barn the pitch of the country and western music rose to a blare, and Max solved the mystery of their source, spying two loudspeakers jerry-rigged near the top of either side of the barn. Presently he was being favored with Bob Wills and The Texas Playboys' rendition of *Big Balls in Cowtown*.

As preoccupied with their chore as they were upon Max's approach, Max could have strode right up to the two men completely unnoticed. One was a near giant, six-and-one-half-feet tall, who would go 260 pounds if he ate only green leafy salad for a week. The younger man was slightly smaller, but not small.

"Excuse me, but are you Mr. Pa Pat Paul Plymel?" Max intended to ask the older of the two.

"One of us is." Pa Pat Paul answered in *basso profundo* without looking up. He was dressed in typical work clothes; slacks, and a shirt, work boots. His graying blond hairline was receding in the front, and longish on the sides and back, Pa Pat Paul was always much too busy farming and railing against pesticides, herbicides, and hormones to give himself over to frequent tonsorial attention. He had the weathered face of someone who had battled for years all that Mother Nature had dealt him, and now was battling human made pests that were packaged, sprayed, injected, and fed. He was in no mood to be interrupted by anyone curious enough to know his view on those subjects, but too lazy to pick up a newspaper and read them.

"My name is Max Markhov, and I would just like to speak with you for a few minutes about your positions on the use of artificial ingredients in farming." It was then that Max saw for the first time exactly what sort of teeth clipping the woman in the house had meant. Pa Pat Paul and Pat Paul were clipping the needle teeth of newborn piglets. This was not an uncommon procedure among pig farmers, done as a prophylactic against the piglets injuring the mother sow while they were suckling, or their siblings when fighting to be the piglet to suckle the milkiest teat. Pa Pat Paul was using a pair of side cutters, a small tool that resembled a pair of pliers.

"You from the Department of Agriculture?" Pa Pat Paul asked indignantly, still not deigning to look at Max.

"No sir. I'm doing research for my employer. We're hoping to obtain the source of all positions on the controversial issues that concern you, and some of yours seem extremely informed."

Pa Pat Paul, holding the side cutters in one hand and steadying the piglet with the other asked incisively, "Are you from one of them IMC outfits?"

"Yes, I'm with Guardian Enterprises, LLC," Max answered truthfully and unadvisedly. At that, Pa Pat Paul turned to face Max, and began slowly to approach him, glint in his eyes, side cutters in one hand and piglet in the other, stepping off as if in a western movie shootout in the middle of a dusty main street.

"Now you listen to me boy, and I'll tell you my views and then you're gonna get the hell offa my property. My views are that IMC and anyone in cahoots with IMC are nothing but a bunch of poisonous rattlesnakes, and on this farm we shoot to kill any snakes we see." Pa Pat Paul began to pick up the pace, dropping the pliers, but keeping a hold on the newborn pink porcine, which had begun to squeal in its confusion. Max began to backpedal, hands held up and outward in a defensive position, recalling Algie's admonishment that he should strive to avoid conflict and confrontation with Pa Pat Paul, as if the farmer's stature alone would be insufficient cause to discourage that.

"I've got nothing to say to you, but turn around and go back to your snakes at IMC or Guardian or wherever, and tell them I'm coming after them and ain't gonna stop, never, and sending spy boys out to see me makes me wanna try even harder. Now git!"

Pa Pat Paul was in full stride now, grasping the little piglet in his right hand by the animal's hind legs, oblivious to Pat Paul's cries of "Pa, the pig, the pig!"

Pa Pat Paul could move pretty good for a man his size. Yet Max had the benefit of youth and his workouts in the gym, so he managed for about 50 yards to maintain a few strides lead on Pa Pat Paul as he raced for his Schwinn. Then, home field advantage told and Max, looking back to see if his pursuer was still in the chase, tripped in a washed out rut, and fell.

He looked up just in time to see Pa Pat Paul come at him swinging the piglet over his head like a cowboy with a lasso ready to rope a calf, while the loudspeakers washed the area with the melody of Patsy Cline's *Back in My Baby's Arms*. The piglet came down hard upon Max's head and shoulders, two, three times again, squealing all the while, but not much worse for the wear, physically if not emotionally.

Max was able to upright himself and resume running the last a hundred yards or so to his bicycle, all the while hearing in his ears Plymel's deep voiced human howling and the piglet's high-pitched squealing, the high end of the register making as much sense to Max as the low. Finally, he reached his bicycle with a sizable lead on Pa Pat Paul, who then abandoned his pursuit and began to beat a strategic retreat, cuddling his baby bit of livestock in his arms and giving it small, apologetic kisses on its head.

"I'm back where I be-long,

Back in ba-by's arms."

CHAPTER 13

Mel had just pedaled past the entrance to the Cumberland Lakes Apartments and began carrying her bicycle through the doorway. She had been ruminating on the inexplicable observations, and trying to theorize about what it all could mean. Something had ripped off her supernova, was chewing off an entire petal of the White Rose Galaxy. Even Doc T.A. was at a loss. Could it be. . . . .no. She instantly discarded every hypothetical as it occurred to her. As she turned to close the entrance door behind her she looked up and saw Max approaching on his bike a couple hundred yards in the middle distance. As he neared, she could begin to discern something amiss with his appearance. As he dismounted and walked his bicycle up to her, she could see that his shirt had been torn, scuffs and dirt on his shirt, face, and trousers, and some small abrasions on his face.

"What. . . . happened. . . .to. . . . you? Mel asked.

Max negligently dropped his bicycle, and pushing himself through the front common door of their fourplex shouted, "I've been pig-whipped!"

. . . .

Mel caught up to Max in time to see him discard his shirt into the wastebasket, drop his drawers, which were salvable, and leave a trail of tee shirt, underwear, and socks, on his route to the shower.

After Max had showered, dressed and regained relative calm, he sat down on the sofa with Mel. She deferred the first word.

"Damned hayseed assaulted me. Algie won't like that but what could I do? Wasn't going to lie to the old fool."

"Who assaulted you Max?

"This Plymel fellow. He's a farmer. The one I *t-o-l-l-l-e-d* you about, but you *ob-viously* don't remember. Algie wanted me to find out more about him that could be useful information for opinionizing his facts that he writes in the newspaper. He resented my association with GE and IMC, to put it mildly." Max took a drink of ice water, and paused, leaning his head on the sofa back.

Mel approached gingerly. "Should you report this to the police?"

"Absolutely not! Algie would explode." Max sprang up, agitated again. "Bad pub for GE. No, we have to let it go."

"Well," Mel was roused by the sight of her Max being harmed, "this should tell you something about GE and IMC. Maybe it's time you reconsidered your position there."

"Melibea, this pig farmer, this Plymel, he's a WWP Democrat. I wasn't assaulted by IMC Republicans. I was assaulted by the other guys. I can't say for sure about the pig."

Mel found herself in a hole, so she stopped digging. "Let's stay home tonight and make a pizza together. We haven't done that in ages." She popped up from the sofa. "I think we have everything we need. What do you say?"

"Sure, sounds good." Max sipped another swallow of ice water, and placed the cold glass on his forehead.

CHAPTER 14

Yet for all the political persuasions of Pa Pat Paul Plymel, Max continued to be conflicted about his employment, and struggled to ignore the possibility of quitting GE. The pay was decent, he had even been able to salt away a few bucks, but was the money worth more than all the rest?

True, also, was that Mel's growing preoccupation if not obsession with whatever had suddenly started consuming PGC6240, had taken away from Max more and more of her time. She had been all about her own work, and had less and less time and thought for Max. Mel had been spending more time at the planetarium than at home or anywhere else with Max. She felt some guilt that she never even remembered that he was assigned to investigate this Plymel fellow, and hadn't even had time or interest to ask him what he'd been up to with his work. Science is a jealous mistress, for sure.

Thus Mel and Max continued the status quo, plodding along in their relationship like two athletes trying to run in deep mud, until two weeks later more data was received from Henrietta. The void, as measured by Henrietta seeing the surrounding objects as well as the mid- and far-infrared radiation emanating uniformly from the outer extremity, was determined to be growing at an alarming rate, and beginning to take on an irregular, oblate shape, like a large portion of hot wax bulging outward, as it was telescopically observable from Earth orbit or from Earth's southern hemisphere. Brainstorming for plausible hypotheses, however flimsy in these initial stages, Mel and the others of her team had, cautiously and with qualifications to protect their reputations, posited that the bubble, its new working title, was perhaps the birthing of a separate universe bordering our own. Whatever it was, it had now grown to approximately 60 light years across at its widest point, and its forward edge had approached to Earth by another approximately 38 million light years. All calculations incredibly indicated that the bubble's rate of expansion was much faster than they had ever before measured it, and faster than the laws of physics allowed. The bubble was approaching into the direction of our own Milky Way Galaxy at the rate of approximately 200 million light years per solar year. At this rate it would reach Earth in approximately one-and-one-half solar years!

Soon, word of the menacing bubble found its natural path into the public discussion, and international media headlines from around the world.

In Berlin:

Ist die Weiße Rose Galaxie verschwinden?

In Mexico City:

¿Qué está pasando con la galaxia PGC6240?

In Rome:

Gli astronomi dicono qualcosa sta consumando la Rosa Bianca Galaxy.

In Moscow:

Астрономы говорят куски Белой Розы *Galaxy* отсутствуют.

In Paris:

Un trou est en croissance dans la galaxie 6240.

But the inimitable British tabloids, never to be outdone, topped them all:

Loony Uni 2 Is Loose!

Nor was Doctor T.A. Banks immune from the journalists' interest. Wishing to hold to a minimum the time spent away from her work, she granted an exclusive interview to the state's largest newspaper, but no others. Thus it was one day she invited into her office a bright young man youthfully attired, with a necktie that had been many times loosened, and hung on a bedpost in his bedroom, but never completely undone since it had been tied for the first time. The necktie was askew when he entered Dr. Banks's office.

"Of all the earthly phenomena we can suggest to give you some idea of what the bubble resembles, we would say a bubble rising on the top of a thick tomato based sauce cooking in a pot on your stove. But this bubble is not perfectly globular, but it jiggles as it expands, which causes it to have wider areas and narrower areas." Dr. Banks's compassion reminded her that this nice young man was not a scientist, and most of his readership were not scientists. She endeavored to answer in lay terms whenever possible to do so without compromising scientific accuracy.

"Is this a black hole?" the journalist, seated comfortably with pad and pen in his hands, recorder recording, asked the one question that had by then become *de rigueur*.

"Oh no. The bubble presents itself to be nothing at all like black holes. The density of a black hole is so powerful as to pull into it anything within its vicinity. Nothing can escape a black hole, not even light, hence the name. But this bubble, and that might no longer be the best name, exerts virtually no effect on the space nearest to it, immediately adjacent to it. It has no apparent gravitational attraction. The bubble does not to the slightest degree affect the movement or orbits of any object however close to it. We have by infrared heat observations noticed only slight temperature change close to the bubble. In fact, we have even observed light from stars within a few hundred thousand miles from the edge of the bubble and, far from being sucked into the bubble, we can observe the starlight shining on the bubble's dark surface, as our sun's light shines on the surface of our moon. In short, except for the malignancy of the bubble's growth into the space already occupied by a heavenly body or any other matter, as well as some intermittent, weak GRBs—I'm sorry, gamma ray bursts—coming sporadically from what seem to us to be random points on the bubble's surface, and as one-time events even at those points, the bubble seems to be entirely benign.

Once the bubble does move, however, everything in its path is consumed or disappears, choose your own word. Our problem, or better to say our challenge, is this: the bubble is expanding at a rate of speed far exceeding the speed of light, and, in our direction, which means the bubble is catching up to us as measured by both time and space. Do you remember from your childhood the fable of *The Tortoise and the Hare*?" He was a nice young man. Perhaps their talk would interest him in becoming an astronomy student, Dr. Banks thought.

"Yes."

"Well, suppose we tweak the fable a bit. Let's say the hare early in the race is a mile ahead of the tortoise as measured by space, and at the respective rates of speed the two are traveling, say, five minutes ahead of the tortoise in time. But then, suppose this tortoise is a supernatural tortoise and starts running even faster than the hare." Dr. Banks raised her eyebrows, waiting.

"The tortoise will catch up to the hare."

"He will catch up to the hare as measured by space *and* by time; soon he will be only one half mile behind the hare as measured by space, and *less than* two-and-one-half minutes behind the hare as measured by time. Soon the tortoise will collide with the hare, sharing the same space and the same time.

"Since this bubble is expanding faster than light speed, and in our direction, it is catching up to us. It is closing the space distance, *and* the time distance between us. So what we saw it doing through our telescopes the first time is what it was doing 340 million years ago, that is, at a distance that light can travel in 340 million years. The last time we saw what the bubble was doing, it had done what we saw it doing only 300 million light years ago, at a distance it takes light to travel in 300 million years. You see?"

The journalist removed the pen from his lips. "But how can that be? I thought nothing in our universe could travel faster than light. That's a basic law of physics. True?"

"True enough in *our* universe. But one working hypothesis we have is that what is inside this bubble, if there is anything inside this bubble, is part of a separate and discrete other universe; a universe with physical laws other than our own, or boundaries to its laws that exceed those of our physical laws, or physical laws that quickly expire or mutate rapidly, or perhaps no physical laws at all to speak of, at least not at this time, or while this phenomena has been observable from Earth." Dr. Banks was grinning girlishly at the idea of an anything-goes universe.

"Trying to assess another universe by using the physical laws of our own is rather like trying to close our eyes and then put human clothes on a creature we have never seen before, when we don't know if the creature has human form, or if our clothes will be the right fit for the unknown creature, or even if the creature wears clothes, or knows what clothes are.

"The phenomenon in this bubble may be another universe undergoing its own cosmic expansion, as ours underwent cosmic expansion in the microsecond after the Big Bang. Then, our universe expanded from the approximate size of a pea to the size of a basketball. But don't feel tied down to our time or our size. The size of the other universe's basketball could be the size of our entire universe or even larger, for aught we know. And after all is said and done, time is simply the way we humans measure change. If nothing ever changed, the concept of time would be meaningless gibber. So a phase transition that lasted a mere microsecond following our own Big Bang, might be a phase transition in the other universe that lasts what for us are eons.

"Have you any other questions? I could go into bubble nucleation if you are interested?" Dr. Banks hoped the young journalist would be interested. He had nice blue eyes.

The young reporter had stopped writing. His eyelids were retracted and his nice blue eyes were protruding. "Umm, no thanks. I think I have enough for my story."

CHAPTER 15

"Thank you for coming up to see me this morning Melibea." Trail greeted Mel at the door of the latter's office. Won't you have some tea and cookies from the table. I baked them myself. Old southern recipe." Trailing Arbutus Banks shuffled over to the table. "Please do sit down. We have something important to talk about, and I need your help." Mel took a seat and a cookie on a napkin and poured a cup of tea. Trail had already partaken.

"Thank you Dr. Banks."

"I've told you before—it's Trail. Especially when we are alone. You are a Ph.D. as well, or have you forgotten? And you have become so invaluable to me. Now, more than ever."

"What can I do for you, Trail?"

"The *Académie* has met via videoconference regarding the bubble—such an uncomfortable name, it pricks me every time I pick it up—and what science must do about it, and do at once."

"What can we do?" Mel asked, knowing that there was so little information about this discovery.

"Why, what science always does, look for and find some answers. Only then can we develop a remedial measure to this menace. But all of that will cost money for research, and more money for development, providing we do find answers." Dr. Banks poured herself another cup of tea. "So the *Académie* members resolved to seek public and private funding sources from all quarters in our membership's respective countries to begin the research into this phenomenon at an unprecedented level. It is to be an international effort, but the cost will be enormous, and funding must be procured as quickly as possible."

Dr. Banks assumed the role of student, knowing that Melibea had undoubtedly been theorizing while the *Académie* was videoconferencing. "What do you think this massive, exploding bubble is? Tell me. Any possibilities?"

Mel finished swallowing a bite of cookie. "These are delicious."

"Thank you. And your scientific answer would be?"

"It sounds crazy, I warn you, Trail."

Dr. Banks leaned her head back and laughed aloud. "Melibea, what could sound crazier than some of what we already know about the observable universe?"

"Well, some of us, some of us in the team, have taken the fact of this bubble's inflation rate, how unthinkable is the speed of its increase, and we've posited that perhaps, just perhaps, it is some second universe that is being born, one that is too close for comfort to our own, and that it is undergoing a gargantuan phase transition as it is born."

"If that sounds crazy, then the overwhelming majority of the *Académie's* membership is crazy with you for that is precisely the theory we have reached, at least for a starting point. As a matter of fact, the *Académie* found the word bubble too undignified a moniker to hang on something so profound. What we are seeing is '*alia universum*'—roughly translated as another universe.

"Dark energy you are familiar with, I know. It is an intrinsic, fundamental force in our universe, and it makes up about two-thirds of all the energy in our universe. But what if, in the alia, this other universe, that has so aggressively introduced itself to us, dark energy is more than two thirds, up to one hundred percent of what is there, presently, anyway?"

"Then," Melibea tried to follow, "the negative pressure in the already expanding universe would continually accelerate, and accelerate to. . . ."

Dr. Banks stepped in. ". . . .pretty much however fast the alia might continue to move towards us, at least until some sort of matter, is created within the expanding energy, which in turn would create some sort of gravity, or other countering positive pressure, causing deceleration. And that is where we seem to be. We need to discover some way that we, in our universe, can produce in a closed environment of controlled expansion of dark energy, a positive pressure that will cause it to decelerate.

"But it has been only in the last decade that we have been able to finally replicate in laboratory experiments an artificial type of dark energy, a quintessence, which is a type of fundamental force. But if our theory holds water, it is akin to the fundamental force, the dark energy of this other universe, and we could use our experiments as a model to develop a positive pressure, and we might then be able to actualize some means of inserting it into the alia to catalyze the creation of the positive pressure to work against the dark energy's negative pressure. Another cookie?"

"No thanks. They're too good. More tea, please.

"But Dr. Banks, Trail I mean, since it appears that this universe, this alia, whose birth we are witnessing is consuming all the matter of our universe that lies in its path, would it not be reasonable to assume that as it consumes more and more of our universe's matter—stars, galaxies, even galaxy clusters, all of which of course have mass and therefore gravity, which is another fundamental force of nature—that that gravitational pull, once inside the alia which previously contained only dark energy, will provide the positive pressure to cause the inflation to slow or stop altogether?"

Possibly. Your question raises questions. First question: Is the alia universe actually ingesting the matter from our universe? We think so. Were it destroying the stars at the point of contact, we are almost certain there would be spectacular visible evidence of such phenomena. Second question: If the answer to the first question is yes, and if the alia is presently nothing but dark energy, and as large as it appears to be, will the gravitational pull of the matter it ingests *be sufficient* to slow its rate of expansion? Third question: Have we answered all the previous questions correctly? Bear in mind, the only astrophysical tools in our toolbox are tools we developed by learning how *our own* universe behaves. We have no way to know as of now what makes the alia tick. Is there gravity there? Throwing gravity into it might work, or it might be as efficacious to feed it cooked cabbage.

"In any event, all we can do is all we can do. And all we can do right now is research in an effort to find a solution. Doing all that will require time, and will cost untold sums of money. Just one experiment with the artificially replicated dark energy in the laboratory expends half a dozen medial trifequessent receptors, and they are not cheap or easily built."

"How can I help you Trail? You know I would do anything I can."

"Go with me to Washington. As the *Académie's* senior member from the United States, it is incumbent on me to seek emergency funding here. I have arranged to meet Representative Carlton Hindman of Texas, who happens to be the Chair of the House Appropriations Committee. We will broach this subject to him in his office, and if all goes well, he will schedule hearings to begin the process of receiving some government outlay of funds for the research we need. This might not be an easy sale, especially since we already asked for and received considerable funds from Washington to help deliver baby Henrietta. You could be an immense help to me in Washington, Melibea," Trail implored.

"When do we leave?" was Mel's answer.

. . . .

A week later, Trailing Arbutus Banks and Melibea Paz were passengers together on the flight to Reagan International Airport. Mel took the window, Trail the aisle, seat. Once in the air, the two began to review notes in preparation for meeting Congressman Carlton D. Hindman. Trail and Mel had a foreboding that convincing Rep. Hindman or even making him understand the need for this crucial scientific project might be a daunting task. They might have despaired of even making the trip had they known so much as Rep. Hindman's acquaintance with science extended only so far as a "D" in high school chemistry, and his casual observation of the anatomy of mule deer he had shot dead, strung up, and field dressed.

The plane touched down in good time, and Drs. Banks and Paz were driving away in a rental to their hotel, nearby the Rayburn House Office Building, where they were appointed to meet a compact Texas tornado.

CHAPTER 16

At ten-o'-clock sharp the next morning, Trail and Mel were seated across from Hindman's oversized wooden desk and his oversized leather upholstered chair in his oversized wood-paneled, wainscoted office trying to explain to him, among many other things, astronomical distances in every way they thought he might understand. Their student was a 72-year-old Texan with as many years spent in congress as Trailing Arbutus had spent in astronomy and astrophysics. He was maybe two inches taller than Trail, and like her couldn't care less that his physical size was diminutive since he measured himself and others more by their abilities and not at all by their physical challenges. As a matter of fact, Trail and Carlton also shared the bias of giving more respect to those who in life had had to surmount physical challenges, as opposed to those who had always enjoyed the privileges accompanying the possessors of physical attributes that are accepted as being desirable only as a result of irrational social constructs. Rep. Hindman also wore eyeglasses for his advanced myopia, eyeglasses which he habitually put on and then removed, pushed up on top of his head, and then pulled down over his eyes, up, down, on, off, up, down, on, off. Carlton Hindman's head was also as hairless as a bird's egg.

"Well I don't know parsecs from parsnips, but I know this much," it was Carlton's turn now. "Before you go asking the members of my committee for their approval to give you science brainiacs two billion dollars or thereabouts that are as good as already earmarked to go elsewhere, you'd better come up with a place in the budget to find the money so no additional taxes are needed, and then find a reason better than there's a big ol' bubble way out yonder in outer space and you need the money to buy a needle to pop it." Carlton had another habit of emphasizing his points while speaking by repeatedly and simultaneously jabbing his two index fingers into the air before him. He was jabbing away at Trail and Mel to beat the band.

Mel was deferring to her elder colleague who sat placidly waiting for the tornado to blow out. At some length, Trail was able to interject herself into a monologue that had once been a conversation.

"Mr. Chairman, if I could just direct your attention to these enhanced images of PGC6240 or The White Rose Galaxy as we sometimes call it, which we have blown up to poster size, you can see better the expanse of what you called the bubble, or as we now refer to it, *alia universum*, the other universe, and how large it is. We have drawn a red circle around the black area that was the petal of the rose but that has by now been consumed by the alia. If you will look at the figures at the top of the blow-up. . . . "

Carlton picked up his eyeglasses in his hand, placed them over his weak eyes, and walked around the desk to the edge of the table where Melibea had placed on a portable easel a photo Henrietta had recently made. Glasses off again, he leaned over to within a few inches of the poster to peer at PGC6240.

"Why, I wish you'd look at that." Glasses on again. "It does look like a white rose! Say, you ever see my wife's white roses?" The congressman stepped lively over to his shelves full of the normal photos showing a member of congress with whomever doing whatever, and, glasses off again, reached for a framed 8"x10" color glossy of a cluster of white rose blossoms. "Here they are." He handed the photo to Trail. "She's won the Blue Ribbon two years running at the state fair. Won't let me near 'em to even give 'em water. Says I wouldn't do it the right way. She's probably right about that."

Trail and Mel respectfully allowed a quiet moment as his beatific smile widened while he gazed upon his wife's prize winners. "They are beautiful," Mel said, fraternizing. Trail sighed audibly and touched her bosom with a hand as if to acknowledge she was beholding a savior born.

"Yes." The congressman pulled his gaze away from the flowers and his smile turned to a frown. "Damned flower thrips give my wife the dickens though. Did you know they'll eat up a whole rose in one morning? Imagine that. She made her own homemade spray mixture though, and she's fought them to standstill." Carlton replaced the holy photo on his shelf. "Did you know a thrips has the option to reproduce sexually or asexually? Can choose either way. Given the choice, it sounds like a no-brainer to me," he said to Trail with a sidelong wink and a half-mouth smile.

"Congressman, could we look again at *our* rose?" Trail gently touched his forearm.

"Oh yes, sorry professor."

The trio returned to the easel and the photo of the damaged galaxy.

"It's eaten a whole petal, has it? Imagine that." For once the congressman gazed at The White Rose with a serious expression of consideration which lasted all of five seconds. Then he said, "You don't think there might be some monster alien thrips out there chomping down on your rose?" His seriousness turned to laughter, and Trail and Mel knew their time there was being wasted. After some brief summation by Trail while Mel packed up the blow-ups and easel, Trail thanked the congressman for his time and once again urged him to schedule hearings. They approached the oversized door that communicated with his outer office space.

"I'll see what I can do," he chortled after the two women. Trail and Mel left after exchanging good-byes.

CHAPTER 17

"Phyllis it has been so good to see you, and let's not make it as long until we see each other again."A well-dressed light haired man in his forties, with a wiry toothbrush moustache, who appeared to be younger than his years, was shaking Phyllis's hand in preparation for taking his leave. The man was Dickenson W. Ferguson, President of Interstellar Forward Assets, Inc., an IMC Corporation.

"So nice to see you, Dick. My feeling is that we will see each other again soon if this item before Carl's committee is as significant as you describe it to be. Please give my regards to Maureen and the children. I still can hardly believe how they've grown."

"S'long Phyllis."

"Good-bye Dick." Dickenson turned and carrying his homburg hat walked out the office door.

Phyllis genuinely liked Dickenson, or at least his intellect which she found to be on a par with her own. Phyllis had listened to Dickenson for the past half-hour or so describe how funding was being sought by scientists for research and later development of a response to a threat of some sort they perceived to be developing in space. The request was going before the House Appropriations Subcommittee on Commerce, Justice, Science, and Related Agencies. At the same time, Interstellar Forward Assets was also seeking additional large sums to subsidize its further development and construction of a fleet of spacecraft that could have both civil and military applications for the ongoing colonization of Mars, and outward exploration from its Martian base. IFA's requests were before the same subcommittee. Dickenson was pulling out all the stops to forestall any competing funding from leaving Chairman Carlton Hindman's committee, and he had been bending Phyllis's ear to make sure she did her part.

What Dickenson did not know, and did not learn in his meeting with Phyllis, was that Phyllis had been in communication with Carlton Hindman about the issue of scheduling committee hearings on the funding request for counteracting the menace of the bubble, or, as it was now more properly called, *alia universum*, growing out of PGC6240 for some days now. Dickenson was a businessman, an exceptionally good businessman, but only a businessman. He had no time or taste for government or politicians and when he needed something from them, Interstellar Forward Assets' President would go to GE, and at GE he would go to Phyllis.

So Phyllis had kept her hole card face down in the recently concluded meeting, and that card said that Phyllis and GE, and Carlton Hindman for that matter, were already on board with seeing to it that what was worrying Dickenson would be bottled up in committee until Carlton Hindman's wife stopped growing roses. Chairman Hindman had cooperated with his IMC and GE managers by arranging to slow walk the funding request through normal appropriation procedures, not as emergency funding. There was any number of agenda items that IMC would prefer to use taxpayer money for besides protecting planet Earth. But Phyllis never thoughtlessly tossed away advantages, and so in this recently concluded conversation she had allowed inference to be drawn that what she would do she would do for Dick.

. . . .

Algernon Amberguese hurried himself down the leafy corridor of the 9th floor of the Guardian Enterprises, LLC, building to the spacious corner office of Phyllis Winders, GE's Government Adjunct Department Director. His rumbling G-I tract was churning, delivering up and delivering down, small, gaseous expulsions from his body. These latest issued from his mouth and provided him with slight taste sensations evoking a feeling of nostalgia in Algie for the filling beef and bean burrito—*La Tonelada* – and the two Sonoran hot dogs he had conquered at lunch. He sported a trencherman's souvenir of the dogs' condiments near the bottom of his purple striped necktie.

Algie was back in the fortress again less than one hour after Phyllis had caused Algie's videophone to provide the patrons in Umberto's Restaurant a few bars of Rimsky-Korsakoff. Algie was compelled to return the call only immediately after winning one large battle in his victorious war against the finest Sonoran hot dogs anywhere he had seen, which is to say consumed, north of *baja* Arizona. Phyllis telephonically commanded an impromptu audience with Algie as soon as he could return to the office, her office, and that is where Algie with his gas was walking now. As he approached Phyllis's professional confines he met walking toward him a neatly trimmed pale, blond man of middle years, sporting a moustache, wearing a pin-striped suit, stickpin, two-tone wingtips, and carrying a homburg. The stranger to Algie said Hello to Algie, and Algie burped out a salutation in reply.

Phyllis's office door was closed; it was always closed. Algie paused in front of the door for a moment to extricate his handkerchief and give a brief wipe to his hands and brow. He knocked three times, carefully, with not over-much authority.

"Come in, Algie." Phyllis knew these things. Algie went in.

"Please do sit down, Algie." Algie sat down. Phyllis was already seated at her desk, flanked on either side by two long rows of cacti sullenly soaking up the sun on the window ledge behind and on either side of her. (Phyllis Winders was not an aspidistra kind of woman.) "We have been monitoring something recently. It's tugging at our pant legs, and doesn't appear to be going away, so we need to amply resource it beginning now. Something out of the ordinary, so we will probably need to study up to the learning curve. What does your unit know about outer space?"

"More than one might expect," replied a person with years of accreted skill in his chosen profession. Although he hadn't the foggiest notion of how much those in his Unit knew of outer space, he was sure that someone, somewhere would expect someone in his Unit to know less on the subject than he or she really did know, thus he knew a safe answer to give without missing a beat.

Phyllis pierced Algernon with her stare for a few seconds, unsure if his answer was concordant with her question, before continuing, "Well and good, because Carl phoned me this morning. He was swinging from the rafters about more and more pressure being put on him in the past couple of weeks from the scientific community in and out of government to hold committee hearings on something happening in outer space that some are saying could threaten Earth." Phyllis picked up a manila folder and tossed it to the far side of her desk, at Algernon. Algernon reached for them, interested in the contents because Phyllis was interested in the contents.

"No need to read them now. Those are back-up hard copies of everything I've already sent you as attachments you'll find on your computer. I had plenty of time to do that—you were at lunch." Algie noticed a tartness in Phyllis's tone when she observed his absence while seeking gustatory pleasure. "You will see in there everything that your Unit needs to start. These white smock people are clamoring for money from congress to study something so far out in outer space that not even your voice would carry there." Algernon's facial expression did not even twitch when for the second time Phyllis seemed to append to her remakrs gratuitous asperity concerning him. People had said his voice carried. He made another mental note to tone down his voice. "IMC doesn't want this money spent for public science projects. IMC's corporations need as much money from the taxpayer as they can grab to help pay for IMC's Interstellar Forward Assets' R&D for expansion of its near-Mars orbiting satellites and defense initiatives, and what the white smocks are asking for threatens to blow a hole in that money. Carl and our other co-op offs on his committee need the goods to loosen up the scientific facts being laid out by this bunch." Phyllis was finished, but she had learned it would be considered courteous to wait now for Algie to respond briefly and satisfactorily before dismissing him. Algie, however, had wandered into the manila folder.

"Algie, you can peruse that later. I know you have your Unit meeting to attend at two-o'-clock," she glanced at her small desk clock, "and you wouldn't want me to detain you."

"Thank you, Phyllis." That was sufficient closure, so thought Phyllis, and she rose abruptly. But Algie added a brief coda. "This could be more interesting and more challenging than anything my Unit has tackled, but we will tackle this." Phyllis had already begun walking to her door, and Algie followed suit, suppressing another gaseous eruption, seeking an exit from the nether regions this time.

As Phyllis was escorting Algie out of her office, and Algie was escorting the file folder out of the office, Phyllis added, "A perfect starting point for you would be a professor right here at our university. Her name is on the top there," Phyllis pointed to the file: "Dr. Trailing Arbutus Banks."

CHAPTER 18

Mel was at the planetarium, her otherwise agitated mind soothed by the steady rainfall outdoors like a slow roll played on snare drums. She and Max had seen each other in but small snippets of time since her return from Washington. She had not had time to talk to him about her trip, nor he to talk to her about any progress, if it could be thus described, in the Plymel matter. They had expressed mutual regrets of that deprivation of their communion and exchanged promises of talking and being together more as soon as the current urgencies of work abated. Their communication, what of it there had been, had taken on a formal sound.

Mel could see that the scratches on his face had healed. But a kiss in passing is no substitute for a long talk while lazily cuddled together abed on a rainy day. She determined that she would spend time with Max that very evening for sure, come what may. They would do the first thing Max suggested, so long as it would be done together. Maybe if the rain slackened. . . .

Tip entered the planetarium, his usual self possessed, beaming expression of having awoken again this very morning to discover this world as the best of all possible, and the other person in the room as the best possible fellow one could meet in the best possible world. Mel knew for certain that Tip would cheer her up in some way, a small joke, a kind word, some completely innocent observation about the trivial that would once again strike a chord in her that would make her whole psyche respond positively. She was unsure if she would like for that to happen just then. There were some considerations she had let lay half hidden, half buried in the sands of avoidance, considerations that she would perhaps force herself to face soon, but at a time of her own choosing, and when she would be alone.

"Hey team leader, or should I say 'Washington Insider.' *Como te va?* Great to have you back. Have any luck winning Congressman Hindman's support for funding our teeny-tiny project to save the world?" was Tip's first question.

"Hi Tip. I'm well. Good to see you." Mel smiled instinctively. Never had she felt other than happiness upon seeing Tip for the first time in the day, and was happy to see him now. He could be a distraction from work sometimes, yes, but she was learning the truth to the adage that no time spent doing something one enjoys is ever wasted. "No; no luck with Congressman Hindman. Would've had better luck asking him to support funding to eliminate the flower thrips."

"The who?"

"Never mind. Here," Mel nodded toward a small gift bag on the table a few feet from her, "that's for you. Dr. Banks and I had about an hour to wander near our hotel before catching a cab ride to the airport, and we ducked into a small curio shop."

Tip smiled a prolonged smile at Mel and then at the gift bag. He opened the bag and then unwrapped the colored tissue paper to see two small plaster busts, one of Sir Isaac Newton, the other of Galileo. Tip stared at them for a moment or two and then looked up at Mel, into her brown eyes, and Mel held his gaze, looking into Tip's, and each wondered for an awkward moment what who would do next.

Mel had brought Max a necktie from the airport.

. . . .

"Oh, good. I was hoping to find both of you, and here you are." Trailing Arbutus Banks pattered into the room, turning Mel's and Tip's head, rescuing them from an awkward uncertainty. Tip pushed the busts back into the gift bag.

"We have just received the latest findings from Henrietta and Cerro Tololo, and they mutually corroborate that the alia's rate of expansion has continued to increase." Mel for the first time saw Dr. Banks appear drawn, tired, a little rattled and unsure of which words to choose. "What has happened is that which all of us had feared, but were reluctant to even discuss. The alia has been accelerating, and now to an alarming rate. The alia, as recently as we can see it, is pushing itself right in the direction of Earth and is now only slightly more than 150 light years away. At this rate it will envelop our solar system far sooner than we had calculated, in less than one year."

"But. . . .we have no way to know if its rate of expansion has not increased, or will increase, even more than it has in the more recent past. If that is true, it will reach our neighborhood in far less time; three months from now, a month from now, or. . . .if it continues accelerating its rate of expansion there is no evidence to disallow the possibility that it could catch up to us in time and space and devour our little corner of the Milky Way as we are sleeping in our beds tonight."

Dr. Banks looked silently at the floor, arms crossed, lost in thought. Mel and Tip looked at each other with aspects quite unlike those their countenances had shown only two minutes before. Then, Dr. Banks looked back at her younger colleagues, reinvigorated by her remembrance of what must be done. She placed arms akimbo, and then raised and smacked the back of her right hand into the palm of her left.

"Yet, the worst is only a possibility; we don't know if it is even probable. It is equally reasonable to hypothesize that this other universe's outlaw rate of expansion will slow, that the energy fueling the inflation will gradually or evenly abruptly expend, relieving some stressors by giving us more time to find how to counteract its destructive movement with positive internal pressure or otherwise. In either event, we have only two choices: we can keep trying, or we can quit. I have chosen, and I know I need not ask either of you if you would choose to quit. So, we must push harder to procure the research funding needed. The situation is most urgent. Science has no understanding of the fist that may be about to punch us in the face. And we cannot stop a threat we don't first understand."

"What's our next step, Doc T.A. You know we are going to do everything we can." Tip offered.

"I have set a face-to-face meeting tomorrow with our local congressman who is home for a two-week congressional recess to meet with constituents and show himself around the district. He also sits on the House Appropriations Subcommittee that will be hearing our funding request; fortuitous for our cause, no? Please, both of you meet me in my office tomorrow afternoon at four-o'-clock sharp."

"We'll be there."

"Of course, we will."

Dr. Banks thanked them and then turned to leave, but then reversed step and said as an afterthought, "I'm afraid other of the team members have dropped off from this project. They were reluctant to come to you first, Mel. They had signed on to find a supernova, not go into some sort of alternative universe speculative cosmology."

Trail smiled and turned away returning to her thoughts and her office. Tip and Mel looked at each other.

"She's so strong. Stronger than I am. I have needed her so much in this past year, and now she is starting to need us, Tip. If I could only. . . . . . " Tip put his arm around Mel.

"Mel no one has worked harder on this project than you, not even that lioness who was just in the room. You have worked virtually non-stop for a year. Have you ever had any diversion in all that time?" Mel's silence said no.

"Mel," Tip turned Mel to face him. You need a night out, you and Max, together that is. You have to replenish your soul. Spend four hours with friends doing something trivial and being entertained. There's going to be a campy new musical revue singing at *The Woebegone Wobbegong* this weekend. They call themselves *Bubbly Effervescence and the Cork Poppers.* Everyone who has seen them says they're worth ten times the ticket price. Why don't you and Max meet us there Saturday evening around six? Mel, you need to do this. You are not a machine." He gently squeezed her arms for emphasis on his last point.

Mel said what she knew she must say. "I think you're right Tip. I'll talk with Max tonight. We should be able to make it. Thanks." She reached, gave, and received a warm embrace that for that moment met the needs of two.

CHAPTER 19

Algernon Amberguese raised his hands in front of him and replaced his handkerchief into its customary reticule, and stepped into the room containing the seated members his Public Policy Support Unit, and without wasting time on prefacing remarks or frivolous greetings commenced the weekly Unit assignment meeting.

Jerry was first in line to receive a new work detail. Algie dished out to him something touching and concerning land use issues in the state's two southernmost counties; issues that if not favorably disposed of would hurt the people (by hurting IMC development), that would create hundreds (a few dozen) of new good-paying (mostly minimum wage) jobs for people in the state (existing IMC employees).

"Max, first of all, good work on the Plymel matter. We've already begun distribution and marketing of your material opinionizing his positions on agricultural practices. The gemstone was that he still practices clipping piglets' needle teeth, which some quarters view as inhumane and unnecessary. We can derive a lot of mileage from that."

Max sat uneasily. "But that is unrelated to his positions we wish to destroy, his positions against the beneficial herbicides and pesticides and hormones produced by IMC corporations."

"Matters not," Algie shook his head forcefully while gulping bottled water. "Calling into question his humane treatment of his own livestock undermines the public's sympathetic perception of anything he says. Not fair? Boo-hoo-hoo. Humans don't reach conclusions dispassionately except perhpas in mathematics. When it comes to public policy, you give them a calculator, and I'll give them imagery, and I'll take any bet you wish to lay that they'll see things my way and not yours.

"So Max, I want you and Ayesha to do a little follow-up on Farmer Pa Pat Paul in archives. I know there surely must be additional ore to be mined there; find it and we'll hit him where he lives."

"In addition to the pathos we have used to soften up the image of the good farmer, we now need as much research produced by our IMC-paid chemists and plant specialists to go with Max's splendid work in time to respond to his latest diatribe in the local rag. Phyllis has already called the publisher and played the fairness card. So we can respond with a lengthy piece on the op-ed page as soon as you compose an outline to be fleshed out. So Max, you and Ayesha work on that together.

"But first Max I want to pair you with Jerry to work for a while on this land use problem, which is boiling over right now. You and Jerry are excused from the rest of the meeting to start on this. Off you go" Algie paused while Max and Jerry excused themselves from the room. Algie replenished himself with another gulp of water, licked his lips, and gathered his next thoughts.

"Ellacinda, have you hand-held Senator Wattkin Crottels through his tax credit reduction bill long enough? If you have, there is something bright, shiny, and new for you."

"He's comfortable with the direction we've given him." Bespectacled Ellacinda sat up, reflexively placing her fingers on her computer keyboard, at the ready to memorialize all the importance that might come her way in the next moments. "The bill has been referred to a more friendly committee, largely because there is now a perception that more study is needed to determine what the possible consequences might be if the bill is passed. That's a perception we created! Hooray for the home team!" Ellacinda was nothing if not efficient.

"Splendid." She had told Algie what he had expected to hear. "Then now it's on to bigger and better things for you Ellacinda, because at GE more is expected from those who do more. Some of you might have caught a word or two about some astronomical findings suggesting or claiming that there is some bogeyman in outer space coming our way. These scientists have banded together and their coalition members have dispersed around the world, tin cup in hand, trying to cadge money from governments, including our own. That is money that by all rights should be going to IMC.

IMC Republican Congressman Carlton Hindman—you know Chair of the Appropriations Committee—called Phyllis and is feeling pressure to schedule hearings. Our Hindman now feels he is going to have to have subcommittee hearings on the subject before he soils his pants, if he hasn't already. Phyllis wishes—and a Phyllis wish is what to us?—everybody:"

"Our Command," the Unit, absent Max and Jerry, spoke in unison.

"Ellacinda, one of the ringleaders of this scientific cabal is local, a professor at the university's exalted Astronomy Department, a Dr. Trailing Arbutus Banks. Start with an archive dive and see if you can resurface with anything. This will be a challenge unless you're some whiz bang physics geek. You're not one of those too, are you?

· · · · · · · · · · · · · · ·

Mel pedaled home to the Cumberland Lakes Apartments after ten-o'-clock that night. Passing through the main approach to the housing complex she noticed the backlit sign identifying the place, and that some waggish vandals had salaciously insulted the natural beauty of the name by removing the "BER" from the signage letters.

She was mentally fatigued. So fatigued mentally that she had not the energy to be frightened of what might be, either on or away from Earth. She was a problem solver by nature, but she felt like she was trying to solve an equation that had too many missing numbers, or read a page in a book that had too many missing letters. She must find those before she could even begin to solve the problems. And now time for that must be given over to lobbying congress for needed funds. Plus, her team membership had dwindled down to where it was not but two two three besides her and Tip, since the others had lost interest once the petal of The White Rose disappeared. And she and Max. What there? She must sleep now, if sleep would come, while the time available to solve both problems was fast slipping away.

She saw the light in their apartment was still burning. She slowed her bicycle, dismounted and carried it inside. Walking in, she saw Max sitting at the sofa. All was quiet, and he did not stir.

"You're up late, stranger. GE give you the day off tomorrow?" she propped her bicycle against the wall, and Max turned to her.

"Oh hi. No." he forced a smile, rose, and went to her, kissed her. "Just thinking about work. Not good to do, I know. But you do it so much that I figured it might be worth a try."

"Ouch." Mel grimaced. "But I guess I deserved that. Speaking of which, let's both quit thinking about work and go for a night out this Saturday. You work tomorrow and Friday, and so do I. Tomorrow Trail and I must cajole a local pol to support funding. But Saturday night," she took Max by the hand and led him to the sofa to sit next to her, "there is going to be a musical group performing at *The Woebegone Wobbegong*, and I'm told they are out of this world. A few of the gang from my Department and some others are going, but I promise—no shop talk. Just a night of fun, friends and campy entertainment. Please Max, let's go. We haven't done something like this for too long. It's just what we need." Mel looked at Max, offering up to him all the hope that was in her heart.

"What's the name of this musical group?"

"*Bubbly Effervescence and the Cork Poppers.*" Mel raised her arms above her head and snapped her fingers, clapped her hands in a mock dance.

"Oh, believe it or not, I have heard some people at work say some good things about them. Saturday night?" Mel nodded vigorously with a nascent smile beginning to show.

"It's a date." Max put his strong hands behind her neck and pulled her to him, kissing her, telling her silently what she needed most to find answers, to solve one problem, the one much nearer.

CHAPTER 20

"This Representative Goodson is much more your contemporary than mine, Melibea. So it would be better if you did most of the talking, I think. And by the way, when we go into his office, before you start, let's look around his office first to see if there are any photographs of flowers lurking on walls or shelves," Trail added satirically. Trail eased her electric car into the parking lot of the office mall owned by WWP subsidiary Professional Properties, Inc., and containing the suite rented for a dollar a month to Rep. Tony Goodson, WWP's cooperating office holding Democrat, and a hometown boy. Tip had been unavoidably detained from joining Dr. Banks and Melibea and couldn't meet with Goodson.

Representative Goodson was a rather conservative WWP Democrat, situated in a swing district that cleaved along lines formed by the social issues that Algie had accurately said mattered not to either IMC of WWP, but did matter to the voters in Goodson's district. Both parties needed to field a fiscally conservative candidate, which Goodson had proved himself to be. The district, however, could be captured by either party only by using a candidate who could walk a very narrow political chalk line of moderateness as bland as a baby's pablum. One toe placed over either side of that line would mean serious damage inflicted by an outrage of moral opposition from the left or from the right, depending. Were it possible, and it very nearly could be possible, with the help of guidance from both IMC and WWP, a candidate for this seat would go through the entire campaign speaking tens of thousands words and when ballots started to be cast, still be an unknown quantity.

Rep. Goodson had what used to be called matinee idol looks, back when there used to be matinees. He was young, 32, and a married father of a boy and a girl. His wife was a Sunday School teacher of children, and the daughter and granddaughter of Protestant preachers. Tony was admired for his high tenor, and he and his wife both sang in their church choir. The couple saw life as a Manichean struggle against the forces of evil, a struggle from which she especially did not shrink. She was an asset to Tony, a real vote getter. Once elected, Tony could not or would not do much to advance an agenda that would mean a toe across the chalk line, but he also would not buck his wife, and implicitly supported her in her causes, however, cautiously and in ambiguities expressed with comforting words. And then, back in his home district, he would place blame for his inefficacy squarely where it belonged, as always, the forces of evil. We must keep fighting harder, so vote for me again, was the biennial refrain.

"Yes, thank you. We're here for an appointment with the representative. This is Dr. T. A. Banks, and I'm Melibea Paz."

"*Dr.* Meliba Paz," Trail hastened to add.

An innocuous staffer actually on the payroll of the congressman's *government* budget, was summoned by the receptionist, came out smiling and ushered Trail and Mel into the Representative's private public office. The congressman gave them fully 20 minutes of his valuable time. 20 minutes given to two constituents was not in his calculations an economical expenditure of time while home, even when given to a constituent as renowned as Dr. T. A. Banks. Besides, he already knew from Hindman and his WWP-paid staff why she would be coming, and what her spiel would be, and he had already determined that his default position, the cautious, earnest, uncommitted concern, would be the best. Still, he knew of other

WWP Democrats on the House Appropriations Subcommittee who had found a way clear to support the requested funding, or were wavering. So he had to wear a mask expressing extreme interest and solicitude, and more than his ordinary degree of caution and non-committal. He left them with his final word that presently he could promise only to give serious consideration to funding what impressed him as a potentially grave, but unproven and controversial, scientific theory.

Trail and Mel left the office. 20 minutes given to one mealy-mouthed congressman had not been, the two of them estimated, an economical expenditure of their time. Trail and Mel knew what they were facing was no theory, and had heard no controversy spoken over it, although they soon would. But still, from the tidbits of information, rumor, and educated guesses, Trail and Mel figured the balance in the subcommittee, and if the effort reached that far, the full committee, could be determined by a few as two votes, and one of them Goodson's.

The committee hearing would be in less than two weeks. While waiting for updated information from Henrietta and Cerro Tololo, they must prepare for a barrage of questions from 13 members of congress about a subject they could not explain fully even to themselves, and Trail would be trying to convince those members of the wisdom and prudence of approving a recommendation for funding research into it. Trail would be walking onto a testimonial battleground carrying a blunted sword and no shield.

CHAPTER 21

Mel and Max were pedaling the final city block approaching *The Woebegone Wobbegong*, the smell of rain in the air which met their faces gently in the sweet evening. They had spoken easily and lightly to each other on the way, about their town, about landmarks, places they had been and agreed they should visit again, the trivial and the commonplace, and about *Bubbly and the Poppers*. Max said coming was a good idea. Mel voiced her agreement, but as their destination hove into sight the thought suddenly occurred to her that she couldn't figure out what she was doing. She was sure that whatever it was would make her feel better, would cheer her up, and maybe help her and Max's relationship. But *what was she doing?* Was she taking Max to *The Woebegone Wobbegong*, or meeting Tip there?

The Woebegone Wobbegong was an unpretentious corner establishment located off-campus, but nonetheless a favorite among students, undergraduate and graduate alike. Unknown to most of the patrons of *The Wobb*, it had been built in 1901, and its original business was an undertaker's office and funeral parlor. Now, some 140 years later, the business there was still embalming people, only live ones, and only partially, temporarily, and gradually, each night. The exterior of *The Wobb* was red brick from the original construction, now painted white, with two large, etched plate glass windows facing the sidewalk with beer advertisement lights blinking out at the public. Blue awnings extended down and out from the top of each of the two windows, bearing interlaced *WW*s on them. Between the two windows were double, wood-framed doors with the name of the establishment painted on the doors' windows in gold bordered, red serif lettering. Above the door, and running the length of the two large windows was a blinking sign done in multicolored neon and illuminating the name *The Woebegone Wobbegong* and complementing neon flashing lights of a forlorn-looking cartoon shark on either side. A large plastic sign was rope tied just below the sign announcing a two-night, weekend performance of the one and only *Bubbly Effervescence and the Cork Poppers.*

Inside, *The Wobb* was spacious, containing a number of square feet that most first timers thought were deceived by the exterior appearance. The original brick exterior facing walls had been restored to the rustic red seen by the early 20th century passersby. There was a foyer past the entrance doors, restrooms on either side, and ramps on either side, leading down to a sunken table area. Stairs from left and right of the foyer led to varnished wood balcony seating, opened for crowds whenever needed for popular live entertainment. They were needed for *Bubbly Effervescence and the Cork Poppers.*

Straight ahead was a curtained stage, before and during performances lit by half shell foot lights around the apron. The wooden bar was to the left as one entered, and ran the length of *The Wobb*, with stools aplenty.

Tip had purchased a table of tickets for the group with Mel fronting him funds for her and Max's seats. Tip had done well, reserving a table near the stage. In the party were Mel, Max and Tip, two others from the Astronomy Department not involved in the effort against the *alia universum,* and a graduate Sociology student, by the name of Martin Jayce. Mel was happy to see the latter, and immediately decided she would become extremely interested in Sociology as soon as the group sat down. Thereafter, if the conversation drifted to freshwater lakes in South America, ancient

Babylonian artifacts, or anywhere else but Astronomy she would do her part to hold up her end of the conversation.

The happy party of revelers took seats at their assigned table, and in no time a newly minted Philosophy B.A. stood tableside ready to take drink orders. Beverages on the way, the companions began general light conversation. Everyone knew, or was at least an acquaintance of, everyone else, but for Martin, the graduate Sociology student, who knew only Karen Niemeyer, his friend and another astronomer. The others were naturally eager to become acquainted with Martin, and to that end most of the early conversation made Martin the center of attention for the asking and giving of information. After the first round of drinks, this was done, and the conversation became more sufficiently lubricated.

After the second round of drinks had been delivered, the anticipatory crowd was becoming restless to hear and see the night's entertainment. "Bring out Bubbly! Bring out Bubbly!" chants went up in the air. Then, as if on cue, the lights dimmed, and the curtain raised, and a professional, *par excellence,* all drag queen revue was revealed, with Bubbly Effervescence standing in front of her three back-up singers, all dressed to the nines, and ready to step off at the sound of the first note of their small band they had brought in tow.

All of the group was decked out in matching sequined and feathered tops, fishnet stockings and heels, and feathered head pieces. All wore wigs of different bright colors. Bubbly's wig was blue, while the Poppers wore a red, orange, and green wig. The stage makeup was tastefully but liberally applied for the dual purpose of the band's own identity and the brightness of the Fresnel lights beating down on the "girls." Red rouge worn abundantly, long fake eyelashes, glittered eye shadow, and, of course, apple red lipstick, all shown brilliantly in the lights.

As a lengthy welcoming applause was dying, the leader of the revue stepped a few more paces forward toward the audience edge of the apron, and signaled the start of the first number with a flourish of her over-sized ostrich feather hand fan. The band struck the first notes of *I Will Follow Him*, the show was on, and the audience was in for a treat like nothing at all nearly anyone in the crowd had ever seen.

The opening number was followed by *He's A Rebel*, which had Bubbly vigorously discard her ostrich feather fan, and *Ain't No Mountain High Enough*. Then, Bubbly and The Poppers exited and the band played a short rift of contemporary tunes. When they had finished and received polite applause, a small violin section joined the band, the Fresnel lights were killed, and a spotlight came on to illuminate the star of the show as she entered stage right, revealing a quick change of costume. She was now in a mauve, ankle length, high waisted, a-line, chiffon dress, colorfully embroidered across the neckline, and wearing a brown wig with braids resting down the front of Bubbly. With an abrupt change of tempo, the violins opened softly, and spotlighted Bubbly Effervescence, and for all the while she gave her adoring fans a more than creditable "Lauretta" singing *O mio babbino caro.*

Every patron was by now enchanted, thrilled and electrified, but none more so than the owner of *The Woebegone Wobbegong.* The bartenders, including extra part-timers brought in for reinforcements, were scurrying mightily to stay abreast of the orders. Alcohol fueled tips were carried away by the servers, and the tip jars at the bar were ostentatiously stuffed to overflowing. Mel and her group were enjoying the show immensely. Mel and Max, the couple, felt a resurgence of their relationship's earlier days, but Mel cautiously considered if it were real or artificially produced by the evening's atmospherics.

The first set of songs ended with a bang-up rendition of *Single Girl*, which at its end had the tables erupting in deafening applause, and those in the balconies stomping on the wood floors. It was a minute or two after the curtain had lowered before the normal din of the night club was heard again, and conversation at the table could resume, but only at an above normal pitch.

"Oh my God, I'm exhausted, and I never left my seat!" Karen thrilled.

"I have never in my life been so entertained! Weren't they fabulous Max?" Mel grabbed Max's hand, and he was beaming.

"They were amazing, all right." Max said, gently rubbing Mel's back with his arm extended around her.

"Hey, let's not forget the band. They were worth the price of admission by themselves!" Tip added. "How about you, Martin? Did you enjoy the first set?"

Martin was reserved, but since he had been asked, he offered, "They're always at least terrific, but I've seen them better."

"You've seen them perform before?" Mel asked.

"Sure have. Two performances before tonight, plus a rehearsal."

"But I heard that all rehearsals are absolutely closed, that Bubbly's and the Poppers' out-of-character identities are strictly guarded secrets." Tip said.

"Yeah, that's what I know." Karen said. "How did you get into a rehearsal. Do you know one of them personally, Martin?"

Martin took another swallow of his fifth gin and tonic. "In a way. I'm a singer myself. Bubbly auditioned me a while back when one of the Poppers left to do other things, and he—or she—needed a replacement Popper. I wasn't offered the job, but I did catch a quick peek at the real Bubbly. You'd be surprised if I told you, I'm sure." Martin swallowed another drink of gin, and then stopped talking.

"Well you have to tell us now, Martin." Karen insisted. "Who is Bubbly really?"

Martin paused, eyeing the others at his table, hesitating. "She's some politician from here. Name of Tony Goodson."

Mel and Tip shot a discreet but meaningful glance toward each other, but said nothing.

"Well that's boring." Karen harrumphed. "I thought it might be someone I know."

"Sorry to disappoint. So let's change the subject. Enough about all that, and you've already heard about my Sociology studies. Tell me all about your astronomical work." Martin steered the conversation into the one subject Mel had successfully avoided so far. "Heard you're working on some pretty important things that might be interesting to hear all about."

Tip, who Mel had enlisted as an ally, endeavored on Mel's behalf to strangle the subject in its crib, citing the undesirable necessity of going into the deep weeds of nerdy astrophysics, and his need for some diversion, but Karen and Martin were having none of it. Tip gave Mel an apologetic look, and started giving short answers to direct questions.

Mel would not feed this topic. "I'm going to use the restroom before Bubbly and her girls start up again. Do you feel the need, Karen?"

"I'll pass," Karen said to Mel looking at Tip. Mel left the table and the astronomical Q&A between Karen and Tip had evolved into a general discussion of the strange expanding universe that had captured everyone's but Max's attention.

When Mel returned, the conversation was still in the stars. Mel leaned over and planted a small peck on Max's head. By then, Karen and the other astronomy students were seeking elaboration on the laconic answers Tip had been stubbornly surrendering to them. Mel felt politeness obliged her, and once drafted, unwillingly entered the discussion. She surreptitiously glanced at Max who had by now begun to become sullen, silently staring at his drink, the stage, the walls. He was stuck in that gear the rest of the night, and she couldn't really blame him, as the conversation never returned to something he could relate to so he could join it. Mel tried, but the group stared glassy-eyed when she mentioned Max's work at GE, and Max was helpless to go into much detail about the confidential work he did at the fortress anyway. Then the house lights dimmed, the curtain raised, and the color, sounds, and magic of *Bubbly Effervescence and The Cork Poppers* resumed with the second set. But there was, for some, at one table, less magic to be felt in the second set.

CHAPTER 22

As the crowd emptied from *The Wobb*, ears ringing with the night's musical spectacle, Melibea and her little group exchanged parting comments and pledges to see one another again, and then went separate ways. Mel and Max pedaled home slowly, and carefully, in prudent consideration of their slightly inebriated state. Max kept the lead, and Mel followed, and conversation along the darkened street was nearly non-existent after the first two blocks.

Late the next morning, a Sunday, Mel woke up in an empty bed. Not unusual, she thought. The bedside clock told her it was nearly ten. She raised herself out of bed, went to the bathroom and stepped into the shower stall. After a nice wash, she dried and dressed and went into the main room to see Max. He was dressed and hunched over the kitchenette counter, scribbling a note on a pad. His backpack was hanging from one shoulder.

"G'morning. You're going out?. . . . Working on Sunday?

Max looked up, not smiling. "Oh, good morning. I was just leaving you a note that I would be back later today, and we would talk. But you're up, so we can talk now."

Mel stepped into the room and sat on the sofa. "You needed to leave me a note that we will talk?" Mel felt an unease arise inside her. "About what? You're going to run away and be a roady with Bubbly Effervescence." Mel assayed an attempt at levity despite her rising apprehension.

"Melibea, we should split up, at least for a while, see how we do apart from each other. We've already been apart from each other mostly for the past several months, we both know that. We've been moving away from each other, living in the same apartment together in a long distance relationship. And I can't buy into the illusion any longer."

Mel sat, stunned. She knew this eventuality had been out there, but never thought it would arrive without more notice, more formal warnings. Or, had she ignored all the warning signals, or been absent when they had arrived?

"You have serious work to do, and you are dedicated to that work wholly, not to anything else, or anybody. I can't be a scientist, and I can't muster enough of what you call social consciousness. I know I have a future with GE; I haven't been given much reason to believe I have one with Melibea Paz. I left my key on the counter next to the coffee maker." Max turned and walked to his bicycle beside the door.

"Max. . . ." Mel stood and started toward him. But then she knew better, knew Max better than that. She had known him to weigh his decisions carefully before taking them, but once having taken a decision he had never altered from the course it set for him. "Where are you going to stay?"

"Jerry says I can bunk at his place for the time being." Max stood his bicycle, and held onto it.

"Max, the work will let up some as soon as we have the funding," she said, unconvincingly to Max, and unconvincingly to herself. Max smiled at her sympathetically, regretfully.

"I wish things could have been different, Melibea." He strapped on his helmet. "We both know now that things between us could never have been different. I really don't want to keep trying, because we both know things would still be just the same as they have been. But I do wish, and I want you to know for what it's worth that I do wish, it could have been possible for things to have been different." Then, Max picked up the Schwinn and turned and silently walked out of Mel's door and life as they both heard the same soft whimper of a dying relationship.

CHAPTER 23

The next several days passed, and Melibea moved through her usual paces—apartment, planetarium, Dr. Banks's office, her two 101 classes, planetarium again, home to bed. Squeezed somewhere in between those would be a sandwich, or a bowl of chili, or a salad, maybe. She had not seen or heard anything from Max since the split, but Tip was there holding her up from time to time when she needed some holding up. She had not raised the subject of her and Max to Tip, and he was sensitive enough to perceive that something adverse to the relationship had occurred, and gentle enough not to ask. He had made his offer previously, and he knew that Melibea knew that he was there for her, available to her.

More than a week after Max walked out the door, Mel was home, having overslept even her persistent snooze button following a late night at the planetarium, when the videophone rang her out of her slumber. It was Trail.

"Oh, hello. Good morning, Trail." Mel began as she pushed herself up on the mattress with one elbow, holding the phone in the hand opposite.

"Melibea, our plane leaves for Washington tomorrow morning at seven-thirty. I'm taking along with us the newest data from Henrietta and Cerro Tololo; we can review in depth together on the plane. The subcommittee hearing will begin at 10 a.m. Tuesday, with a vote on the funding request scheduled for Thursday. I've just been informed that I will be called as one of the first witnesses. Are you all set to go?

"Yes, of course. I could leave in five minutes if you needed."

"Melibea, I have struggled to see through these specimens of the species congressional, and how they will behave in reaction to the external stimuli they will receive this week. As best as I can ascertain, the subcommittee vote will be close among the 13 members, coming down to only one WWP Dem, and one lone wolf IMC Republican. "We'll discuss it more on the plane to DC, but the WWP Dem on the fence is Goodson. He's wavering, but we need something, some clincher, to bring him over. He could be the decider. I keep wracking my brain for something that would make him help us."

. . . .

"Melibea?. . . . . . . Melibea, are you still there?

Mel's presence of mind returned. "Yes, Trail. . . . I'm here. I was just. . . .thinking about . . . . what you said."

. . . .

The tiny little lap trays rested atop Trail's and Mel's knees on the plane, 31,000 feet in the air. The monotonous hum of the engines had faded into the background as the two silently reviewed the latest observations by Henrietta. Occasionally one of the women would point out something to the other, jot down a note or a figure or two, work an equation on a small calculator.

The alia's rate of expansion had continued to increase, and the advancing other universe was now only 70 light years from Earth.

CHAPTER 24

Trail and Mel were breakfasting at a small café next to their hotel before taking a taxi ride to the capitol. There was not much said between them. Trail was mentally preparing, almost meditating, looking vacantly at the plate of food before her. Mel respected that Dr. Banks was about to make the most important presentation of her career, and didn't want to interrupt her with idle chatter, or even speak of the matter at hand unless Trail sought her out.

Their spirits had been buoyed some the night before when word arrived that the lone wolf IMC Republican congressman had declared in support of the requested scientific funding for research and experimentation to develop a response. That, according to Trail's latest count, made the vote as of the morning of her testimony 6-6, with Goodson still an unknown quantity.

"So it appears that our own fiscal and straight-laced conservative Rep. Goodson is going to make or break our request in subcommittee," Trail observed, looking for the server to bring her more juice. "We've tried every tack, every approach to that man, but he remains as inscrutable as the Sphinx.

"Yes, more juice, please." Dr. Banks handed the server her empty small glass. "Have you come up with anything Melibea, *anything*, either persuasion or coercion, we might use upon this man? Our whole project for research and development of some remedy to this existential threat seems to be coming down to this one roll of the dice—Goodson."

Mel kept an anguishing silence, re-crossing her legs, fiddling with her spoon.

"It's nearly impossible to convince some of these members of the gravity of this threat; so much rot masquerading as science is out there. And by men and women who should know better. Some of them former colleagues of mine, whose integrity I would never have doubted."

Dr. Banks was right. IMC, and to a not inconsiderable degree WWP, had been working around the clock to opinionize every comment, present a counter-factual to every article, every utterance in every interview given by the scientific community that was seeking to divert funds away from them and their corporate subsidiaries. WWP sought only to project nuanced differences between its positions and those of IMC so as to remain in a political posture that could pass as a party in opposition to IMC. Media continued churning reports on every position, with equal credence given to all, by reporting all tendered positions and factitious supporting sources from every quarter as factual. Media trembled at accusations of bias from the biased, and rushed to give an appearance of fairness, even to negate the character and existence of truth itself once truth had been simply denied, presenting it as more in the way of an allegation from one or the other side of the fractious issue. All alarm over the *alia universum* that had been sounded had been effectively quieted in the public's ear, a public that had become cloyed, and walked away from it all, to wait until things were sorted out by those who were supposed to know. Thus, incredible as it was, no large numbers of people seemed to be overly concerned about what was headed straight for Earth. Facts and science were losing to cogent and coherent sounding nonsense, delivered by serious non-threatening faces using an earnest tone of voice. The vast majority of the human race was left uncannily unperturbed by the phenomenal threat racing towards them. Life around the globe went on undisturbed, and business continued as usual.

"Trail. . . . ." Mel began to say something, not even knowing what that would be as she spoke her friend and mentor's name.

"Yes, Melibea. What is it? Do you not feel well?"

"This Representative Goodson. . . . ." Mel felt all the blood rushing from her head, a clammy feeling.

"Yes, what of him?" Trail set down her fork, wiped her lips with the cloth handkerchief.

"I found out something about him, about a separate life he is leading. . . . . He's a singer, secretly, in a stage group, with other men."

Mel went on and imparted to Trail the whole story of Tony Goodson *qua* Bubbly Effervescence. Dr. Banks sat silently after listening to Mel finish telling the last of it. After a minute or so Dr. Banks was the first to speak again. She spoke only softly, a brief comment about her scrambled eggs being overdone.

CHAPTER 25

Upon clearing security and finding their way through the corridors, Trail had told Mel to go ahead and seat herself directly behind the witness table, before all the choice seats had been taken. Trail said cryptically that she needed to pay her respects to some of those who had been so much help to her, and then abruptly turned from Mel and was soon lost in the peopled halls of The United States Congress.

Mel found her way to the hearing room and after entering found a seat with a view close behind the witness table. A bank of photojournalists were bunched together facing opposite to the witness table, dressed in casual contrast to the members now arriving in the raised panel above and behind them. Suits and dress suits almost without exception clad the members as well as their IMC- and WWP-paid staffers, the latter assortment mostly young and bright eyed, a few older veterans of many other such clashes.

Some members took their seats and began reviewing documents, a staffer bending over a member's shoulder here and there to helpfully find, clarify, or emphasize. Members would shake hands and have a little private chuckle between them, while some photographer would occasionally take a candid shot portraying what would be perceived, however inaccurately, as government representatives about to do the people's bidding. At length the subcommittee chairman, Representative Nathaniel Crafen, an ancient and respected IMC Republican from Oklahoma entered from behind the door in the wall behind the dais, a tacit signal to all that it was near time to stop all the palaver and look at him lower the gavel in a few minutes.

Then Mel spied Dr. Banks entering the room, laden with her bag, stuffed full with her notebook of opening statement, small computer, and other supporting scientific research which was of utmost importance. She intended to offer into the record all that could not be covered in hearing, none of which would be read, let alone considered by those who were about to compile the record. The documents would be duly and officially entered by a government-paid staffer, never to be seen. As Dr. Trailing Arbutus Banks found the chair behind her name on the folded piece of cardboard, she was disappointed to see that her one simple request for a cushion to be placed in the soft, yielding leather seat of the chair so as to provide her with additional support had not been respected. She had made the request to a government-paid staffer who had passed it on to an off-budget staffer working for the subcommittee chairman, who was IMC-paid. When Dr. Banks sat down in her assigned seat, she sank deep into its plushness. The photojournalists' cameras began snapping away. That afternoon's electronic news broadcasts, web pages, and the next day's editions of print media would show an image of nothing more than a woman's head and her pale lilac scarf around her neck. It could have been a mug shot.

Mel suddenly noticed the absence of Rep. Goodson. This was surprising, and concerning. He was a last holdout and hope for a yea vote. Without his vote, and if Trail's predicted count were accurate, the vote would fail, 6-6. Dr. Banks turned around, and Mel caught her eye. Mel motioned to the dais and pantomimed "Rep. Goodson." Dr. Banks shrugged her shoulders and turned back to the dais.

Following the chairman gaveling the hearing into order, and a few grandiose statements by a couple of the members, the panelists gave their opening statements, pro and con as to the scientific communities request for funding to research and develop remedial action to stop the menace. Then the questioning began.

Questions were directed randomly at the panelists, here a friendly question to a like-minded witness, there a hostile question to a panelist who the questioning member considered to be up to no good. Questions put to Dr. Banks came early, and were not infrequent, as she was known by all to be the lead proponent and for good reason; her credentials were heavily weighted. Some questions were sincere and *bona fide*. Others were not, and some were downright rude and insulting. The first of the latter sort came from the chairman.

"So, Dr. Banks, you're asking us to hit the panic button about an event that happened over 300 million years ago in a distant galaxy, which, after 340 million years, has resulted in not so much as the death of an ant on planet Earth? Can you give me something more?"

Dr. Banks raised herself up to reach her microphone button. "Congressman, what was originally seen was in fact an event that occurred approximately 340 million years ago, but the threatening phenomenon is now much closer to us. Just over 70 light years from Earth." She leaned back and sank down into the leather.

"Oh well, that's practically right next door," the chairman said sarcastically, producing sardonic smiles from others on the committee, staffers and audience. "You know, I woke up today, it was a bright, sunny, beautiful morning. Where is this threat that is so ominous it has Chicken Littles such as yourself coming here and asking for appropriation?"

Trail had to raise herself again. "The threat is real Congressman. The *alia universum* is accelerating. It is moving rather fast."

Congressman Louis Shepperd, a WWP Democrat from Connecticut: "But you just answered the chairman's question that you refer to this thing of yours as "*alia universum*." Isn't that because you don't even know what you're talking about?"

Dr. Banks: "We have a working theory, and based on that theory we believe it is a second universe. Hence, we refer to it as *alia universum,* or simply *alia.* But no, we cannot say exactly. Hence our request to fund further research."

Congresswoman Iris Fisson, IMC Republican from Tennessee: "Dr. Banks, you and your telescopes simply can't see some stars they used to be able to see, correct?"

Dr. Banks: "That's an oversimplification, but somewhat correct, Congresswoman."

Rep. Fisson: "Then isn't it possible these stars just burned out?"

Dr. Banks: "Stars don't just burn out like the light bulb in your desk lamp, Congresswoman." *Lucky for all of us they don't, congresswoman,* Trail thought, biting her tongue.

Congresswoman Esther Dankowicz, WWP Democrat from California: "And you testified earlier that this, bubble—I'm sorry, I can't stop finding humor in that term—is still invading our universe?"

Dr. Banks, on tiptoes: "The alia is not invading our universe, congresswoman."

Rep. Dankowicz: "Then what is it doing to our universe?"

Dr. Banks: "Eating it."

The questioning continued apace for the next hour-and-a-half, Dr. Banks becoming more perturbed with each impertinent, obtuse question. Then her perturbation grew into a more afflicted mental state. Trail was seething inside by this point. The pomposity of these suit shits reading questions that some clever young sophist on their staffs had spun into words to make the responsible, cautious, deliberate scientific method appear like vacillating uncertainty or malicious guessing made Trail estimate that her daily reserve of self-possession had remaining only about one more polite and courteous response to another rude and disrespectful question. She was off her estimate by one response.

"Now, Ms...I'm sorry, Dr." . . . IMC Republican Congressman from Nebraska Nathaniel Thorssen, the most obnoxious in the entire subcommittee, lowered his eyeglasses from atop his wig and placed them over the end of his nose, consulted a written document briefly, and then tremulously read what had been written by Jerry of Max's own GE Unit for him to read: ". . . .Banks. . . . Do I understand that even today neither you nor anyone else in the scientific community can even tell the great American people what is inside your bubble, or what's causing it, or why it is such a dire threat to occasion the expenditure of what could be more than two billion dollars of taxpayer money?"

Dr. T.A. Banks raised herself on her slippered toes sufficient to reach her microphone button, looked directly at the spectacled fur-top, and then the dainty woman wearing the lilac scarf gave a response in a firm voice that would go viral on the internet across the world, an answer entirely responsive to the question and phrased in the literal truth: "Congressman, I cannot today honestly swear under oath that you understand anything."

And with that, the chairman gaveled the hearing to a close.

. . . .

Trail and Mel exited the committee hearing room amid a throng of journalists, photographers, interested parties and other onlookers. Dr. Banks tarried long enough to make a brief comment or say hello to a long-lost friend or quondam professional acquaintance she had not seen in some time. Once in the halls the people were no longer those familiar or concerned with the business that had recently concluded. The crowd was dispersed and Trail and Mel were no longer impeded on their way to the outdoors, another cab ride back to their hotel, checkout, and another cab ride to the airport. Dr. Banks had given it her best, all she had, although she now slightly regretted any abrasion that might have been caused by her final answer. But what's past is past, and the two women were relieved that the ordeal was over.

The plane ride home was unremarkable. Trail was exhausted, and managed to doze and even nod off fitfully, between the interruptions of the normal ambient noise on a flight. When final approach was announced, Mel gently awakened Dr. Banks. Mel had been left to her own thoughts while Dr. Banks dozed, and Mel's mind kept returning to the curiosity of Rep. Goodson's complete absence from the subcommittee hearing. She had asked Dr. Banks about this after the hearing, but Dr. Banks, then among the microphones and notepads and cameras, had only agreed that it was indeed unexpected.

As they were buckling up for the landing, Mel had to ask, "You think Congressman Goodson will support our funding when the subcommittee votes Thursday?"

Dr. Banks reached into her bag and pulled out a small hairbrush. "If he doesn't, I'll bet you a nice blue wig and a pair of fake eyelashes that Bubbly will." Trailing Arbutus Banks smiled wryly, brushing her hair.

CHAPTER 26

As Trail and Mel were in the air coming home, Max had just started to resume his investigation into Pa Pat Paul Plymel in the GE office archives, after he and Jerry had buttoned down the necessary work on the land use bill in the state legislature that was crimping IMC in the southern counties.

He sat down in front of one of the research computers, and was of a mind to start with the computer's alphabetized last name search; the most logical place he knew. He went to that page and clicked on "P" for Plymel. The computer started with the alphabetized list of archived records for any person whose surname began with "P," and Max started scrolling down the list looking for Plymel.

Paciano. . . . . .

Packer. . . . . .

Page. . . . . .

Parman. . . . .

Patterson. . . . . .

Paz. . . . . .

Perlman. . . . .

Perlmutter. . . . . .

P------

"Wait a minute." Max whispered to himself, and scrolled up again. *Paz*. He put the cursor over *Paz* and clicked. What he saw froze him, and as he began to read, knotted his stomach.

Paz, Melibea Calderon: Ph.D., Botany.

Dr. Melibea Calderon Paz, d.o.b. 24 July 2006. Ph.D. in Botany, State University, 2034. Successful Doctoral Dissertation "Affects of Anthropomorphic Climate Change on Plant Physiologies in Tundra Latitudes." Dr. Paz's scientific conclusions deemed to be deleterious to advancement of International Moderators Corporation's profit goals.

Employment at all major IMC public and private institutions of higher education denied, and Dr. Paz's science now highly opinionized, and it's impact negated. See: IMC Guardian Enterprises, Government Adjunct Department, Public Policy Support Unit, Algernon Amberguese.

For additional information, go to:. . . . .

Max could only stare at the monitor. Then his first thought was to close out of the file, and log off the computer. His second thought was to back up and click on Plymel; do what research he came to do, and let the shock wear off. Give no appearance that the information he had stumbled upon had any bearing or relevance to him whatsoever. He had just opened the index to Pat Paul Plymel, Jr. when a cheery, youthful, female voice accosted him from behind.

"Hey Max, you must be here looking into the rube with the nasty ink pen." Ellacinda said demeaningly as she took a seat before the computer next to Max.

"Yep. You got it. Algie really wants to do a number on this guy. You? Working on anything interesting?

"Don't know yet. Could be. Banks, Banks, Banks. . . . Oh there she is—Trailing Arbutus Banks—some name. Gotta find out all I can about this woman. Seems like I remember hearing about her from when I was at the university, but not much about her. I was in the Poly Sci Department." Ellacinda, the human laser beam, intensified, and her eyes neared the monitor.

"Just idle curiosity about a faculty member at your *alma mater?*" Max wanted her to affirm.

"Max you know me, and I never am curious idly. No, IMC has passed word all the way down to GE, and Winders, and Algie that this woman needs to be discredited with every tool at our disposal. I'm one of those tools, and they have disposed me here to the archives.

"OK, here we are." Ellacinda disappeared into her information.

Max logged off. Maybe, he considered, he would take an early lunch.

. . . .

Max pedaled out to the park again, to be among the oasis of trees. The park's support system workers were out, cultivating the trees, bushes, grass; giving water, opening canopies, and otherwise sustaining a habitat for pampered flora and fauna where people loved to visit, much like a zoo without the fences, as these inhabitants were rooted. Max stopped to sit and rest at his favorite thinking spot in the park. He leaned against his friend the sycamore's trunk, and picked up a small piece of plastic litter, turning it in his fingers like a string of worry beads, and stared out into the distance. He was late returning to the office that afternoon.

When Max did return to the fortress, his mind was distracted. Max returned to the GE archives more as a refugee seeking sanctuary inside a building that he really knew he needed to leave entirely. But the archive room was quiet, and most of the employees using it held enough respect for their co-workers' concentration to not interrupt it. Short of just walking out on his job, a decision Max had not reached, this was his next best option for the time.

They haven't really lied to me, Max restarted the mental conversation with himself he had begun at lunch in the park. *Algie and Phyllis have told me all along what GE and IMC do. I knew—or wanted to know—that my work involved providing a counterfactual context. But that wasn't really lying, or was it? Everyone had their own opinions.* Max tapped a few strokes on his keyboard as a lawyer from the Government Adjunct's Legal Unit passed behind him. *But I never thought or imagined—or I didn't want to find out, I suppose—what GE really does, and does to people who stand in its way. Mel tried to tell me about this. And I told her it wasn't these people who had hurt her. I had avoided looking at the truth. I was content not to see the truth. And now the truth has come up from behind, and kicked me in the ass.*

. . . .

It was after six-o'-clock in the evening when Max had an odd feeling as he did something for the very first time; he knocked on the door of his former apartment as a non-resident. And knocked again. Mel wasn't home, or was not inclined to answer. Max had wrestled with his better angels, and they had won. He felt moral compunction for the first time. He had never been a malevolent, hurtful person. Not being mean, not causing suffering to other sentient creatures was just a *modus vivendi* he had adopted, assuming it was the best way for everyone to peacefully co-exist. But that was a morality of refrain; he had not until this moment, taken a significant positive action out of an unalloyed sense of moral right and wrong.

He turned and walked outside to the common area, taking his videophone from his backpack. He unlocked and straddled his bicycle. Before pedaling away he dialed Mel's number, still on his speed dial. The phone rang, and rang, and then Mel's recorded video image and voice invited a message.

"Mel it's me. . . . I'm at your apartment. Just wanted to give you a heads up, but you're not at home. Something I learned by accident. . . .just today. . . . It was Algie and that whole GE bunch that torpedoed your botany career. I was wrong. I'm sorry. . . .And now GE and IMC. . . . .they're coming after Dr. Banks. Just wanted you to know. . . . . I hope you're doing well."

Max rang off, put away his videophone and started pedaling back to Jerry's place. Max's videophone service provider was an International Moderators Corporation subsidiary, ever vigilant in helping to keep Guardian Enterprises, LLC secure.

CHAPTER 27

Mel turned the key in the lock of her little apartment door late the night of her arrival back from Washington. She had been trying to return Max's phone call since after the flight landed, and she and Dr. Banks deplaned, and parted company to seek a long nap after the stress of Washington.

She arrived home, and still no answer from Max on her phone. She didn't know Jerry's phone number. She wanted more of the particulars from Max before taking this to Trail. But the particulars might have to wait. Trail should know what she was up against. She would tell her first thing tomorrow. She dropped her things on the sofa, brushed her teeth, and went to bed, exhausted.

. . . .

Mel's legs pumped mechanically at the pedals of her bicycle the next morning, en route to the Astronomy department to find Dr. Banks and give her the bad news that she was now a specific target for destruction, as if Trail didn't have enough fights to fight already—an alien universe and her own public policy battle against an indifferent if not hostile government, plus being a prime mover in the global effort of the *Académie*.

As she made her way to the campus, it was as if Mel's entire life had become a mechanical function, moving like the gears in her bicycle, not out of choice or desire, but because those and no other movements were possible. The gears had to move in the way they moved, the wheels had to turn in the way they turned, and Melibea Paz had to proceed in the way she was proceeding. She had to continue with the effort to stop the alia, the alien universe; there was no choice. Entire swaths of the southern firmaments had been gobbled up, as if a celestial forest fire had burned through unimaginable distances. Gone were dozens of venerable southern sky spacemarks including entire southern galaxies and galaxy clusters, not to mention the lost petal of PGC6240. And for aught anyone knew, being unable to see what was behind the strange universe, rapidly expanding light years below the southern pole of her own little planet, the entire White Rose Galaxy might be gone.

Mel had arrived outside the planetarium. Her feet had to stop pedaling now, she had to brake her bicycle, she had to find and speak to Trail. She and the bicycle had no choice about what they would do.

. . . .

Mel found Dr. Banks immediately as she entered the foyer of the planetarium.

"Hello, Dr. Paz. My, but don't you look refreshed; ahh, the resilience of youth." Trail walked up to Mel smiling, and saw Mel was not smiling. "What is wrong Melibea?"

"Trail," Mel whispered, "can you come outside with me for a minute?" Dr. Banks could see the seriousness in Mel's face. She followed Mel outside to a small grassy area supported by the university's horticulture projects, where they sat together.

"Trail, Max left me a phone message while we were in DC. It's a warning to us, and to you in particular."

"Oh?"

Mel raised her knees and laced her fingers together around them. "Yes. I think I told you, he has been working at Guardian Enterprises, and, well Guardian Enterprises is owned by IMC. I haven't been able to reach Max yet to ask for more details, but Max said in his message that IMC is coming after you. I can only conjecture that it has to do with our seeking funding for research. We must have placed ourselves in competition against IMC or one of its corporations."

"And how are you and Max doing, Melibea. I've always thought well of him, and you and he seem so happy together."

"We're not together right now Trail. That is why I haven't been able to reach him for more details about this threat to you from IMC."

"You must try to reconcile Melibea. Try everything to save your relationship. It could still work out, and then if it does not work, you will have fewer regrets. But please try everything first before parting ways. Max is a nice man."

"Trail, would you consider ceding the lead role for this congressional battle to another member of the *Académie*, someone from outside the United States? This IMC, they will stop at nothing to destroy you. They destroyed my academic career once already."

"Oh no, Melibea, I could not consider such a thing."

"But Trail---"

"Melibea: I am a scientist. I am not going to ask permission from anyone for how to do science, and I am not going to be intimidated from doing science. Copernicus first sought permission from the church to publish his scientific findings of heliocentrism. Should I seek permission from this, what is it—IMC, to further scientific knowledge, grovel before them like a modern-day Copernicus? No." Trail stood indignantly. "I won't. *Fiat scientia—raet caelum.* No. Don't ask me again."

Dr. Banks stood and brushed the seat of her pants and strode away. That was the first and only time Melibea had been a source of irritation to Dr. Trailing Arbutus Banks. Mel stood and followed Trail back to the planetarium, deeply worried and concerned, but at the same time feeling more admiration than ever for the tiny, petite figure she watched, leading Melibea back to scientific knowledge, and back to her own courage.

CHAPTER 28

When Mel walked into the Astronomy Department conference room the next morning, Thursday, a few minutes past ten-o'-clock, the room was already half full. Two large screen monitors were showing the live broadcast of the congressional channel. The committee hearing room where Trail and Mel had been a few days since looked familiar to her now, and so did some of the faces.

Most of those in the room were from the Astronomy Department, faculty, graduate students, friends, acquaintances. Then Mel even spotted the university president. Nice of him to come.

"Quiet, quiet, it looks like they're starting to actually vote on the appropriation," some attentive soul announced. A gradual quiet settled in the room as the Chairman of the House Appropriations Subcommittee on Commerce, Justice, Science, and Related Agencies had begun to speak. Since the chairman knew that many people would be listening to him speak, he spoke about matters he wanted them to hear him say before turning to matters the people would like to hear, the purpose that had actually assembled the subcommittee.

"Hi, Mel. Moment of truth is here. How do you feel? Any butterflies in your stomach?" It was Tip. He had a cup of coffee in his hands poured from one of the cardboard coffee boxes some generous person had provided, along with bagels.

"By this time Tip, I am resigned to the fates. Of course, I would like for the funding to be approved, but I am not deluding myself about what motivates those people." Mel indicated with a nod of her head at the near television. "The scales have fallen from my eyes."

Others joined Mel and Tip, forming a little knot of her remaining and erstwhile team and supporters who would learn if their funding request would die or move to the next step, consideration by the full House Appropriations Committee.

Someone turned up the volume of the televisions again after having been muted out during the chairman's irrelevancies. The vote count proceeded alphabetically by each member's surname. Rep. Goodson and one other member were late appearing, being detained on the floor of the House by a floor vote, so their names were passed over. The 13-member committee vote reached 6-5 in favor of the funding request, when in walked Rep. Thorsson, who sat down, being told by a staffer what was happening. His name was called and the camera moved to him. Murmurs of "Boooo," broke out in the Astronomy Department conference room. To no one's surprise Rep. Thorsson voted no, making the vote split evenly at 6-6.

"Is Rep. Goodson still detained?" The chairman looked left and right. Does anyone have any knowledge. . . .is he still on the house floor? . . .I know he had a floor vote." The chairman covered his microphone with his hand and leaned back to speak with a staffer. Then someone pointed for him to look to the end of the dais where Representative Goodson's chair was. "Oh, Representative Goodson, how do you do? We're awaiting your vote on the science funding matter. How do you vote."

"Sorry I was detained Mr. Chairman. I would like to explain my vote." Rep. Goodson elaborated about how he had given lengthy consideration to all sides in this matter of a not inconsequential amount of taxpayer funding requested by the scientific community, and, placing hand over heart, begged understanding of how if he would err he would err on the side of preventing an intergalactic Armageddon. With that, Rep. Goodson announced, "I vote yes." His face looked like someone who had just eaten a can of worms.

The request had cleared its first hurdle by a vote of 7-6. Cheers were heard in the room. Mel and Tip hugged. Dr. Banks was at the opposite end of the crowded room with other of the university's leadership including its President. But Mel caught her eye, and saw Trail in a silent salute raise her cup of whatever she was drinking and look at Mel with a knowing smile, touch her hair, and with her free hand give an allusive brush of the finger to her eyelash. *Bubbly.* It was now on to the full committee.

After the climactic vote, the number of people in the room began to dwindle. Everyone's hope and optimism had been renewed. Perhaps they could have the necessary resources after all. If only the alien universe would slow down some, give them more time. But a request for time could not be laid before the *alia universum* as a request for funding placed before congress.

The last persons drained out of the room after about another quarter of an hour. Not unusually, everyone had left it to someone else to turn off the broadcast monitors. No one had, and the broadcasts continued, moving on to a brief local news update. The audio of a news announcer began the second local news story, told to no one in the Astronomy Department conference room. . . . .

A young male body was found floating in a pond at City Park in the early morning hours of today. He appeared to be a white male in his twenties, fully clothed. A Schwinn bicycle and a backpack containing photographic identification of the victim was found at the bank of the pond. Release of the man's identity is pending notification of the family. The death appears to be an accidental drowning, pending final autopsy by the medical examiner.

CHAPTER 29

Dickenson W. Ferguson stood before one of the large windows of Phyllis Winders's 9th floor corner office, turning his hat in his hands. He had just witnessed a near miss in the House Appropriations Subcommittee for Commerce, Science, Space, and Related Agencies, and a man whose business is shooting rockets and satellites up to and from Mars does not take near misses *con salum granum.*

"Dick, this was merely the subcommittee, it signifies nothing." Phyllis Winders was trying to soothe Dickenson W. Ferguson's frayed nerves, and making an honest effort not to be distracted by her admiration of the newly opened red blossom on her cactus that was calmly growing in the window-sill next to the needy flibbertigibbet with the hat sitting next to her.

"It signifies that this science effort to steal tax money, tax money that we should have, is still alive, not dead."

"Dick, I assured you some time ago, and I assure you again, this proposal will not leave Carlton's committee. This is a tempest in a teapot. Nothing more. Algie has been driving his unit on and they are going to stop this appropriation before it reaches the House floor. Did you ever meet Ellacinda Underwood in the Public Policy Support Unit? If we asked her to produce a counterfactual narrative to what we know about the moon she could create a general perception in the world that whether or not it's made of green cheese is just a matter of opinion, and cheese mongers know more about the subject than the lunar colonists and scientists know."

Dickenson hesitated. "She's that good, huh?"

"Better. Now, the subcommittee has done its thing, it's now in the hands of the 38 members of Carlton's committee. We're working it. We'll secure the majority of that committee."

Dickenson had no alternative but to reconcile himself to the efforts and encouragement of Guardian Enterprises, LLC. Phyllis had never failed him before. But still, he thought as he was leaving Phyllis, still, this seems different to him.

Phyllis, now alone in her office, picked up her phone. "Algie!. . . . Forget that! Drop whatever it is you're eating and bring your sorry ass in here! Now!" The one-sided conversation over with a bang of the handset, Winders swiveled around in her chair, facing the windows, her needles bared and sharper than her cacti's.

. . . .

Mel left the conference room and sought out Trail to thank her, and pledge her support for the future battles that lay ahead. She wished she could offer some protection as well, but she had not been able to protect even herself from IMC, so, honestly, what could she do for Trail?

But Dr. Banks was behind closed doors with the university president. Tip had taken the rest of the team back to the computers to consider the latest updates Miqueas had provided. By now, all of the team members besides Tip had become restless about continuing with a project that had so changed since the search began for a supernova. They had lost enthusiasm for becoming political foot soldiers and had either departed or effectively suspended their participation. Mel wanted to join Tip, but had neglected for too long her 101 classes and had no choice but to return to the apartment and grade quizzes and catch up on her lesson plans.

Melibea slowed her bike to the front entrance and greeted nice old Mr. Simmonds, who lived in her fourplex across the hall with his invalided wife. He spoke and asked Mel if she had heard the news about the young man who had drowned in a City Park pond.

"No, I haven't, Mr. Simmonds. How is Ms. Simmonds?"

"She's fine, fine. Thank you. Have you spoken to young Maxim lately?" Mr. Simmonds asked suggestively.

"No," Melibea replied wondering why that would be Mr. Simmonds's business. "Been awfully busy lately." She started to go into the apartment.

"Always admired his Schwinn. When I was his age, I had one exactly like his that my grandfather had passed down to me, same color and all," Mr. Simmonds told her as he had told Max and her only about a thousand times, but this time told her as prologue. "News report said a Schwinn 10-speed was found next to the pond where the man's body was discovered." This gave Mel pause.

"Said the young man was in his twenties, white, brown hair." Mr. Simmonds raised an eyebrow at Mel's back waiting for some reaction that he would never enjoy seeing. Mel continued up the stairs, back to Mr. Simmonds, carrying a bicycle that now felt as if it weighed a ton. She opened her door and placed the bike against the wall, and pulled out her videophone. She checked her local news outlets on the phone. There was a report on the story, corroborating what Mr. Simmonds had said.

She knew. She didn't want to know, but she knew. She didn't need to wait for the identity to be made public to know that much. She knew.

Mel also knew it was no accidental drowning. Max was fit as a fiddle, and a superb swimmer, when he wanted to swim. But Max would no more drop his Schwinn at City Park at three-o'-clock in the morning, and go take a dip in a pond than he would climb a mountaintop and meditate all day and night on how to bring about world peace. He didn't accidentally drown.

Suicide? She had to concede that she couldn't rule it out as a possible explanation, but thought it highly improbable. Not because of her, anyway. Their relationship had been sputtering for some time before the final sundering, and his, and her, acceptance of its final demise had been steadily growing as the relationship was dying. Both had seemed to have become reconciled to being apart.

The one explanation that was predominating over all the others in Mel's mind was: IMC. Max had been working for those ticks for nearly a year now, and all was well with his taskmasters. Until, less than 48 hours after he calls her and blows the whistle on Guardian Enterprises, he is found dead. Suicide? Or IMC? Mel knew.

CHAPTER 30

Three days later, Mel had the medical examiner's report, and the contents virtually confirmed her theory. That the body found floating in City Park was that of Maxim Markhov, she merely skimmed, reading over it as a given. What interested her to see confirmed was found later in the report. The cause of death was not drowning, no. Cause of death was "blunt impact to top of head" with "lacerations and abrasions to vertex of scalp at right frontal and parietal regions." The medical examiner found no evidence of alcohol, or drugs in the body, and no presence of water in the lungs. Max was murdered, and then dumped in the pond. IMC. Case closed, in her mind.

For the first time in her career Mel phoned in to ask someone else to do her job for her. Tip agreed to take her 101 classes this week, and offered to do anything else she needed. He said he would let Dr. Banks know of the situation. Trail and Tip would have to continue the work for a few days in her absence.

And for those next two days, except for one trip to the supermarket's liquor aisle, Mel stayed home and self-medicated. She contended with her feelings of sadness, remorse, and, yes, even guilt. She struggled in her mind to turn over all the facts, and remember. Absolving her in her own mind was the fact of the many times she had tried to caution Max about IMC and its companies, and his rejection and resentment of her Cassandra like warnings. But then, her own moral prosecution would come to the fore and make the case for her condemnation. For just as long a time, and with every warning to Max about IMC, she made clear to him that what repulsed her was IMC's lack of corporate ethics, lack of any corporate motivation besides making more money this year than last, and more money next year than this year. She had preached to Max sermon after sermon about growing his own sense of social justice, and nurturing within himself a guide for his own actions more worthy of allegiance than those of his employer. And was it not her five-year long effort that drove him away from her? And then, after he's gone, the first time he does take a conscience-based decision as she had implored, hectored, and cajoled him to take for all those years, what does it behoove him? He's dead. The medical examiner's report might as well have listed cause of death: Sense of ethics.

. . . .

But, at length, Mel accepted Max's death, and that she must return to her own life. She would not allow herself to become collateral damage in Max's homicide. Nor would she allow IMC to ruin her second career. Nor would she sit passively while they came next for Trail if there were the slimmest chance she could make any difference. So Mel gathered herself together and returned to her research, and brought herself up to date on the science she had missed in her period of political activity and personal grieving. She had now begun assisting Trail in the ramping up effort to obtain full House Appropriations Committee approval, all the while keeping one eye out for any sign that IMC was moving in Trail's direction. And signs there were. Creeping into the public debate about whether to take unprecedented steps against the encroaching second universe, were reports and findings by men and women who had earned their spurs in Astronomy and Astrophysics. All, of course, were educated at IMC universities and in the pay of IMC think tanks, or consultants to organizations that were branches growing on the IMC family tree, not far from the contributing money trunk. The conclusions of these reports were that there was essentially no need to worry at this time. The phenomenon observed—it was finally admitted that it had been observed only because at least that much could no longer be denied—was a naturally occurring event. Take a wait-and-see attitude. The jury was still out. Most disturbing were the attacks against Dr. T. A. Banks's professional position, tinged with insinuations of her creeping senility. The "venerable" doctor, the doctor "whose record in the field of Astronomy dates back nearly to the mid-20th century," exemplified prefaces to many of Trail's observations that would then be doubted and questioned by learned astrophysicists who had more youthful credentials, and implied that science had passed by the previous generation. Dr. Banks and her contemporaries should be honored, but now as debilitated elders, not actively contributing members who were furthering any serious scientific discussion.

CHAPTER 31

As Melibea Paz was pulling herself together, a phone call came to Trail as she was seated in her office, a phone call from her close friend and dear colleague from Chile, Dr. Miqueas de Rojas. He was calling from La Serena. His phone call would inform Dr. Banks of the newest observations from Cerro Tololo and its affiliated networks; observations that would shortly explode, and completely alter the science and politics all across the globe. Dr. de Rojas's image appeared on Dr. Bank's videophone.

"*Buenos días*, Miqueas. I was thinking about you after we spoke two days ago, and how much I wanted to sit with you again and taste the *Caldillo de congrio*, the *chapaleles*, and the delicious *amasado*. Is *La Cocina Serena* still as good as we knew it?"

"Even better, *mi amiga. La mamacita* still makes the *chapaleles* herself, and her grandson, who has been under her tutelage, now is working there under her *ojos vigilantes*. Of course, mostly he wants to make only *los pasteles*." Trail and Maqueas shared a good laugh.

"The way of all youth, no?" Trail laughed again.

"Trail, here at Cerro Tololo we have detected something so spectacular and so wondrous and mysterious, you must know of it at once."

"Has the alia's rate of inflation increased again" Trail tensed to hear the worst.

"Now only 50 light years away. But this news is nothing about the alia, my friend. In fact this is news of an observation made in an area completely opposite the alia, and moving towards us from the opposite direction, towards us, and the alia beyond us. Our telescopes and our affiliated network of southern hemisphere telescopes have just spotted some strange, very bright objects, scores of them, much closer to Earth than the alia is now, but as I said, approaching Earth from the area opposite from the alia. Their visible light has just become detectable. They are moving in a formation, suggesting an intelligent life form. They are presently approximately 45,000,000 kilometers from Earth, and on a course to pass under earth's southern polar region at a distance of merely 400,000 kilometers, and at a rate of speed close to 125,000 kilometers per hour. They are on course and speed to pass directly under Earth in about two weeks."

Dr. Banks had walked over to her office door as she was listening to Dr. de Rojas, and before closing the door, motioned a familiar hand signal with facial expression to the receptionist that meant Dr. Banks was not to be disturbed for anything or anybody until further notice.

"How do they appear to you Miqueas?"

"What they appear to be is a fleet of extraterrestrial spacecraft. But they are flying in formations of 21 craft. Each formation is a shape like an inverted V, or the Greek capital lambda. There is a craft at the point of the lambda, flanked by eight more craft trailing down each side to complete the lambda. Flying inside the inverted V, are four additional craft in a diamond formation. We have counted twelve formations."

"252 extraterrestrial spacecraft."

"Sí, Trail. And each craft is alike, approximately near two kilometers long, skinny and tubular, and curved slightly. Toward the fore of each, the craft separates into two distinct continuation tubes, one on top of the other, that gradually terminate in sharp points. At the stern of each is a circular apparatus attached at points to and surrounding the main tube, and extending beyond that, a final shorter appendage. The upper separation point terminates in a prow that shines bright yellow in color, and the lower terminates in an under prow that will at times glow in reddish-orange. The lights are so bright as to be visible even from earth-based amateur telescopes, and astronomers at several observatories are now calling to us to tell they have seen them, and to ask us if we have seen them, and what do we know. This is why this observation will be international news very soon. As I said, there are scores of them. Many, many bright, shining colorful objects flying in the dark of space.

"Trail, do you know Ibrahim, one of our resident astronomers here?"

"I met him once, very briefly, at your home."

"When we first espied these spacecraft, Ibrahim exclaimed, '*El Zalfiqar Cimitarra!*'" Do you know El Zalfiqar?"

"No, I do not."

"Nor did I, before Ibrahim explained. El Zalfiqar is a famous sword carried by a champion of Ibrahim's faith in the seventh century. Because of the shape of these alien spacecraft we have adopted a name from Ibrahim's inspiration —*Las Cimitarras*."

"The scimitars." Trail whispered into the phone.

"Yes. The scimitars."

CHAPTER 32

Miqueas was not wrong in his estimation that word of the scimitars would soon be international news. The appearance of over 200 alien spacecraft approaching Earth could not be kept under wraps. Unlike some vague astrophysical description of a mysterious force in outer space, people everywhere could relate to, and even see pictures of the alien spacecraft even if they had no access to a telescope. And they were so near; only about 29,000,000 miles from Earth, nearly as close to us as Venus, and headed our way!

Dickenson W. Ferguson acted reflexively, and by the time Phyllis Winders saw him appear on her computer screen, she had already instinctively known what she must do. As was often the case, the conversation was basically Ferguson asking Phyllis to act on the good ideas that had popped into his head, and Winders listening as if she were hearing for the first time an idea that she had not already put into action. This would prove not to be the exception to the rule. After listening to Ferguson explain all that had occurred to him about the ramifications of the aliens' appearance relative to IFA, Phyllis flatteringly told Dickenson how she would get in touch with Carlton Hindman and push him to do just the very things Dickenson had suggested. That conversation between Winders and Hindman was by then already three hours old.

. . . .

"I'm here, Phyllis, can you see me now?" Carlton Hindman was in his office, glasses off, fiddling with this computer's keys, trying this and that to make it work. Hindman refused to own or operate a videophone, or any other technological advancements made since he was a young man. He was most resistant to carrying a videophone, hating to be kept on a tether. Too many people calling with too many bothers. He practiced the art of having everyone leave a message, and then he would return the choice calls, prioritizing those from his beloved wife, Verla.

"Yes, Carl, I can hear and se--"

"Let me try something else. Hold on!"

"Carl, I can hear and see you just fine. . . .Damn!" Phyllis saw the screen image of the Texas tornado spin away into the recesses of his oversized office. Carlton had gone, glasses back on, to summon someone who knew the wizardry of "the buttons."

Next, Phyllis saw the image of a young man peering questioningly at her. "Are you there? Can you hear me?" he asked.

Phyllis took a deep breath, and let it out, slowly. "Yes, I can see you. Yes, I can hear you. Is Carl still there, please?" Phyllis saw the young man move away, and heard his fading voice say it seems to be working now. Then Phyllis saw Carl's potato head reappear and occupy the entire area of her computer screen, as if he thought to improve the reception by moving a few inches closer to her.

"That boy's a genius with these things. Don't know what he did, but here it is working just fine now." The "boy" had sat down and stood up. "You're calling about those spacecraft?"

"Yes, Carl. It occurred to me that they could be our serendipitous good fortune in that we can use their presence to scuttle the science community's funding request and at the same time divert the money to IFA's Mars program development. What you need to do is—"

"You're damn right. Whole town of Washington has its bowels in an uproar. I'm hunkering down in my office. President's over at the Pentagon now, probably picking her toes. Pres' has called a joint session to address the American people about this. That oughta be good."

"Carlton: Stay. Focused. What you need to do is call an immediate full committee hearing, and hold an immediate emergency funding vote on IMF's request for two billion dollars to launch a preemptive nuclear strike against the alien spacecraft from IMF's orbiting thingamajigs. At the same time you will ask for a vote to deny all other regular budgetary funding requests that have been made, including those already approved by your subcommittees, because all resources must now be directed against this newly emerging imminent threat. Dickenson can be in Washington per the time you set to hear the emergency request."

"But I thought we'd already held committee hearings, and Congress had already appropriated those two billion dollars to IMF in our supplementary, off budget, and classified. Hell, DoD has already put those satellites and warheads up there, haven't they?"

"You did, they did, and they are. But no one knows IMF has already received and spent that money, let alone for what purpose, because, as you correctly recall, the money was off budget and classified. That allows us now to make the same request *publicly* for a *different* purpose, since these alien spacecraft are breathing down our neck, and IMF can *then use* the two billion dollars on its Mars program."

"Sounds good." Carlton could connect the dots, so long as there were not too many dots. "But has Dickenson made a request for this?"

"It should be in your mailbox, Carlton. Have you checked your mailbox today while you've been hunkered down?"

"Wait just a minute, Phyllis." Phyllis saw Carlton's head recede and she heard the tornado calling for his young wizard to come back again and push some more buttons.

CHAPTER 33

"My God, it's only seven light years away now." Mel took the news with a gasp.

"And still closing in on us. But, and this is a *big* 'But' Melibea, the silver lining is that the alia's rate of expansion, after having continued to increase, seems now to be slowing considerably and rapidly. We're still running out of time to repel this threat, but not running out of time nearly so quickly, and in fact only very slowly." Trail and Mel were in Trail's office pouring over the newest data from Dr. de Rojas and Henrietta at three-o'-clock in the morning. "It might have now ingested enough of our universe's matter to cause significant positive pressure within. Our theory has new evidence in support."

"Seems to be. Maybe we shouldn't look a gift horse in the mouth, but that seems to be. It reminds me of the ancients' human sacrifices to the gods to appease them." Mel reflected. "We have sacrificed so much of our own universe; entire galaxies: PGC14236, PGC 13853, entire southern constellations are gone now: Dorado, Eridamus, Horologium, Pictor, Reticulum. If it is the matter from our universe that is causing the slowing of the other universe, it's a high price to pay. But worth it, I'm sure."

"Considering the alternative, yes." Trail agreed. "But your wistfulness is not unfounded or maudlin, Melibea. Some day in the not too distant future it will be sad to us in our field, to see so many of our old friends gone now forever. Imagine how those in the art world would react to losing a quarter of the Louvre, or the Hermitage. How would they feel?"

As Melibea looked at Trail, she could imagine how the art world would feel. She could not, at that moment, imagine a not too distant future.

. . . .

The public broadcasting radio news announcer with the sibilant "s" was back on the air, being received in the planetarium's computer room to several listeners, including Mel and Tip.

On Capitol Hill today, the House Appropriations Committee reacted swiftly to the threat posed by the alien spacecraft approaching Earth. Committee Chairman Carlton D. Hindman of Texas called a special meeting, made possible after President Jennifer Oberlander exercised her Constitutional authority and called on Congress to convene an extraordinary session to address the threat.

Speaking forcefully from the dais immediately following a unanimous vote to approve emergency funding of two billion dollars to be used for rapid deployment of the military's thermonuclear assets in low earth orbit, Chairman Hindman spoke forcefully, assuring the American people that, quote "no half measures would be taken against these foreigners seeking to deprive Americans of their American way of life." Hindman later revised and extended his remarks for the record to include, quote, "or any of their ways of life."

The Committee, to pay for this outlay, voted nearly unanimously against the controversial funding request by the scientific community for research into the so-called expanding other universe in outer space, which all experts agree is still light years away from Earth. That request had been approved by the Appropriations Subcommittee for Commerce, Justice, Science, and Related

Agencies. The only dissenting vote against denying that funding came from Representative Tony Goodson----"

"Well that, as the saying goes, is that." Tip said in disgust as he switched off the radio. He wanted to throw it out the window.

"I don't suppose they felt they had any alternative, with the scimitars at our door." Mel responded philosophically.

"We still have hope internationally, but the U.S. was supposed to take the lead on this." Tip grumbled.

"Don't suppose we can do much now except support our allies across the world, and do what little research we can with existing resources. Since the alia has slowed to a crawl, maybe we can renew the funding request after this matter with the scimitars is resolved." Mel was still not ready to throw in the towel.

"Depending on how it is resolved," Tip amended her. "There might not be anything left to worry about after it's resolved because there might not be anything left."

. . . .

Next day Dickenson W. Ferguson, wearing a light green, double-breasted suit, with Kelly green and brown striped necktie, and his ubiquitous homberg, was back in Phyllis's office. Algernon Amberguese was there, standing attentively. Phyllis was composed, seeing clear horizons, and ready to accept all accolades. Thus she was slightly chagrined when the first words from Ferguson were "How about that Carl? He's a wonder isn't he?"

"Yes, he is. A wonder, that's right." Phyllis agreed mechanically, still waiting for the praise to come her way.

"And you, Phyllis. You're prescient, that's the only word. You said that that request by the science nerds would never leave Carl's committee, and by God, it didn't. Prescient, that's what you are."

"Phyllis has been doing this a long, long time, Dickenson. She can predict these outcomes rather accurately, most of the time." Algie said somewhat ineloquently, but not wanting to be outdone in the Praise for Phyllis Department. Phyllis glanced at Algie, unsure if he had not added too unflattering qualifiers to the offerings he had laid before her feet.

"Thank you, Dick." Phyllis basked in the glow. "And you, Algie." She added less forcefully. "So when do you think IFA's missiles will be ready to shoot down these alien spacecraft?"

"Oh they're in position right now. It's up to the Pentagon brass now to call the shot, and once they do, Boom! Bye-bye scimitars! And then IFA can ask Congress for every last dime the taxpayers have to give, and it will be given to us on bended knee with a free kiss on both our butt cheeks."

. . . .

Algie and Dickenson parted from Phyllis after a final word, and strolled together down the 9th floor hallway and to the elevator; two hail fellows well met. Algie wiped his hands with his handkerchief on the elevator before saying good-bye to Dickenson on the 7th floor which held the offices of the Government Adjunct Public Policy Support Unit, as well as its Legal Support Unit. Algie was going into his office door at the same time the surly, beefy male guard Max had encountered on his first visit to the fortress for his job interview was knocking on the office door of Benedict Russell Rembley, attorney-at-law.

"Come in." Rembley beckoned the guard. The guard entered a subdued, darkened office, one with heavy drapes pulled shut, and lit only by two bulbs set in sconces up on the wall opposite to Rembley, and a desk lamp on his desk, illuminating Rembley's face and the several papers and files he was reviewing. Unimpressed with the occupant of the office, the guard disliked all lawyers. His experience with lawyers had been them telling him reasons that he couldn't do what he would like to do. They frequently called it "due process." He would like to do their process.

"Hello Brad, please sit down." There again, a lawyer telling him not to do what he would like to do—leave. Rembley glanced at Brad for a microsecond and then returned to looking at his papers on the desk while he spoke to Brad. He never again looked at Brad for the balance of the meeting. Brad inspected the guest chairs critically, and passively aggressively sat in the second one from him.

"Just wanted to update you on the investigation into that tragic demise of our former employee, what was his name? Markhov? Rembley said, scribbling his signature on the bottom of a page.

"Yes."

"The police still have no leads, and it looks to me like they are running out of stones to turn over." Rembley said. "You can still assure me that you have fully cooperated with our friends in law enforcement, can't you?

"Yes. Absolutely." Brad the guard said, looking at the crown of Rembley's head.

"There's nothing more the police might be able to learn, is there?"

"Nothing. I'm quite sure."

"Yes. So unfortunate. Well, good work, Brad. That's all." Brad stood and walked out into the brightness of the outer world. Rembley never looked up from his papers.

CHAPTER 34

The United States Army's combined military strategic Space and Missile Defense Command, or SPAMDEFCO if one preferred to dip and raise a ladle from the military's alphabet soup, had never been busier. SPAMDEFCO was the most streamlined command in the military, and its satellite system used for detecting and eliminating threats to Earth in general and America in particular was the most advanced and efficient in the world, a fact unknown to but a few inside the military, and Dickenson W. Ferguson to a more limited extent. All military personnel and the small number of IMC civilians working in SPAMDEFCO knew that a loose tongue about his or her work would mean they would leave the comforts of home sweet home one morning and before lunch be looking at the cold confines of their own dungeon without possession of so much as a toothbrush.

After his conversation in Winders's office about IFA, Ferguson traveled directly to an undisclosed location in the Nevada desert. A location undisclosed to Ferguson too. He hadn't known where he was since shortly after leaving Las Vegas. That last leg of the trip he had spent as a guest of SPAMDEFCO, in the luxurious windowless rear of a van that traveled non-stop for three hours, and then released Ferguson into a sealed metal garage that could have housed a four-storey building. Once there, he was tagged, given a civilian visitor card depending from a lanyard that an enlisted hung around Ferguson's neck. This indicated that Ferguson

enjoyed highly classified clearance status, and his presence was to be tol-
erated, and Ferguson watched, closely. Then Ferguson's military handlers
took him to the control room of SPAMDEFCO's 110th Military Defense
Brigade, where he was seated, told that he would be most comfortable in
the chair provided for him. Ferguson sat and was watched.

Colonel Galen Braden, informed of the civilian presence, approached
to confirm and observe. He extended a hearty handshake to Ferguson.

"Good to see you, Dick. The fireworks are about to begin. All set?"
Col. Braden was of medium height, reddish hair, and had a small but
noticeable potbelly. You'll be most comfortable here, in that chair, once the
show begins, which should happen in about 17 minutes. All assets have
been emplaced and General Ziv and I have been in constant communication. I believe you met him once before. He's Deputy Chief of Staff of
SPAMDEFCO Operations. He just confirmed to me again that all tracking
and launch sequences have been programmed. The enemy spacecraft are
being monitored, and we're just waiting to realize the optimum kill shots,
which, as I said should occur in about a quarter hour. Would you like some
coffee or a sandwich?"

"Nothing for me, thanks Gale." Ferguson had started to stand up to
greet the colonel out of civilian politeness, but thought better of making
such a bold, unauthorized gesture. He had been seated, so he sat. "IFA is
confident that the missiles and warheads we have helped provide will be
adequate to the task, and I appreciate the privilege of observing."

"Not at all Dick. We're happy to have you here." Braden said, out of
military politeness. "I've assigned Sergeant Stannis here to be your hos-
pitality host while you're with us. She will make sure you're taken care
of." And watched, he didn't add. "Sergeant Stannis this is Dickenson W.
Ferguson of Interstellar Forward Assets. He gave us the little toys we're
going to play with today."

Sergeant Dorothea Stannis, who was standing at ease a pace behind Col. Braden, stepped one step forward and extended her hand. "We hope when our uninvited guests reach LEO they won't like your toys as much as we do, sir."

"They won't." Ferguson addressed Sgt. Stannis. "But only because they won't be around long enough to find out. They won't know what hit them. That is," Ferguson winked at her, "if your commanding officer's aim is any good." Ferguson was supremely confident in his IFA provided tools.

The scimitars had continued their silent illuminated approach to Earth's underside, and the formations had not altered speed or course since first being observed from Earth. SPAMDEFCO's assets in Low Earth Orbit had the leading formations in the crosshairs, and the 110th MDB's fingers were on the triggers. All was quiet on the space front.

. . . .

In the meanwhile, President Jennifer Oberlander had been addressing the American people from an underground bunker, inside an exact replica of the Oval Office where she had fled with her family, calling on her people to remain calm, and assuring them that the threat would soon be eliminated. No need to panic she assured. She was being watched by all of America including Melibea, Tip, Dr. Banks, and practically everyone else in the Astronomy Department and across the country and the world.

And then, five minutes before SPAMDEFCO's scheduled launch of the warheads, five of the scimitar formations acted. Those five formations were at the vanguard of the entire scimitar fleet. First, they sheared off from the bulk of the fleet to face the orbiting thermonuclear tipped warheads affixed to the missiles. Then the point of each of the five lambda formations silently opened and parted gracefully, allowing the four scimitars in diamond formation inside the lambda to move to the fore. Then the remaining 17 scimitars of each of the five formations assembled into a half circle support formation just behind the four diamond scimitars.

Soon after this maneuvering began, the launch missile order was given from SPAMDEFCO's assets scattered across the western United States, including the 110th Military Defense Brigade's monitors in Nevada, where Ferguson watched. But nothing happened in furtherance of the order. It was as if someone or something had unplugged all of SPAMDEFCO's computers. As a precautionary measure, all manned orbiting activity had been grounded, so as not to endanger those in the vicinity of the thermonuclear explosions that were expected to blast the alien spacecraft to smithereens. And the video transmissions from the military's orbiting communication satellites had gone down with all the other computers. All screens went black and all sensors lost any detectable traces of the attack missiles or the scimitars. SPAMDEFCO was blinded.

Thus, what SPAMDEFCO could not see next was a reddish-orange glow beginning to be visible from the under prows of the 20 scimitars in the fore, all facing the nuclear threats pointed at them. The reddish-orange glow at the under prows of the 20 diamond ships was a by-product of some beam, a beam without any visible or infrared light, gamma rays, or detectable x-ray emissions. That beam had been transmitted to all of the Earthlings' most advanced and powerful type of war craft that were threatening the alien fleet, observational and weaponry.

None of this activity or the activity that followed would be seen or in any other way known by Earthlings for some time later, but they would immediately know that all was not as they had hoped. And it was only some days later, via information from Henrietta, that Dr. Banks and others, would begin to piece together more of the story.

Even if the Earthlings had still had sight to see what would occur next, they would have been disappointed. There would not have been much for them to see, but more than anything else they would see undisputable evidence once again that plans do not determine outcomes. There was no drama, no big fiery explosions, nor any Earthling war craft or scimitar spiraling out of control and down to Earth or out to space. The beams from the scimitars had reached their targets and once they did they caused a force to be applied from the outside of the missiles, satellites, and warheads. This had created a contained high pressure, hundreds of times greater than the pressure exerted at the floor of the ocean beneath the deepest depths, but this was a pressure artificially created and then exerted in a small, circumscribed area in the surrounding absolute vacuum of outer space, and surrounding craft that were designed to enjoy operating in a zero pressure vacuum. The result being that the scimitars simply crumpled the satellites, the missiles and their warheads, wadded up Dickenson W. Ferguson's interstellar forward assets like so many pieces of wastepaper, into little balls, each about the size of a grapefruit, and then flicked them away, far, far away on a harmless journey into deep space at about 150,000 kilometers per hour.

Afterwards, the five vanguard formations reformed into the lambdas, returned to the main fleet, and the main fleet continued on its previous course of approach to the *alia universum*, the immediate puny threat to them eliminated.

CHAPTER 35

Inside the secret 110th Military Defense Brigade's operations command center, or OPCOC, Dickenson W. Ferguson was not seeing what he had expected to see, and did not understand what he was seeing. He was watching military personnel sitting at controls performing first one action and then another, and then speaking to someone else, and then letting someone else try something. He saw Col. Braden communicating with SPAMDEFCO's Deputy Chief of Staff, Gen. Ziv, but he didn't hear congratulatory words spoken. He didn't see smiles or handshakes or cigars lighting up. He was being watched less now, any suspected threat posed by a civilian presence had been eclipsed by the concern for the military's proud space assets being suddenly unaccounted for.

Sgt. Stannis was watching this scene from a somber, stony countenance when Ferguson's concern for his assets emboldened him to pose a question unbidden. "Is there something wrong, sergeant?" seemed to be pertinent and innocuous enough.

"I wouldn't know, sir." Sgt. Stannis dodged hospitably. She did know, but she also knew enough to recognize those occasions when a sergeant shouldn't say what she knows. Then, Col. Braden strode over to Ferguson's chair without intention to stop there. But if Stannis didn't know, Ferguson was resolved to ask someone who did. He even stood from his chair and cut Braden's path.

"How did we do, Gale? Blew those bastards to. . . . " Col. Braden gripped Ferguson's shoulder and without breaking stride answered, "We're still doing a TDA, Dick; oh, a Target Damage Assessment." Braden moved on without looking back. A Missile Disappearance Assessment would have been closer to the truth. Ten minutes later, Dickenson W. Ferguson was back in the metal garage, and then the windowless rear of the same van, and less than three hours later the Las Vegas airport. He boarded the next flight home, and when wheels were up he still knew nothing of any TDA.

. . . .

After the truth had gradually come filtering down to the Earth's surface and known to all, a general perplexity overcame the minds of the Earthlings. The Army's communication satellites and missiles with nuclear payloads were gone, where and how it had happened was unknown, but they were most assuredly gone. But, on the other hand, the scimitars had left Earth's vicinity as well, and were speeding away as fast as they had come. So the Earthlings did not know which side had won the game, or if the game had merely ended in a draw. No one knew if they should panic or celebrate. No one that is except a tall Black woman in a corner office in a secured building hundreds of miles from the 110th Military Defense Brigade's home base.

CHAPTER 36

"We're still here, and they're still there." Trailing Arbutus Banks said, an observation which just about summed up the *status quo post hoc*. Melibea Paz, and Ernst Tippleskirchen were gathered in the planetarium. They were, indeed, still there, like the rest of the world was still where it had been prior to the noiseless, one-sided, space battle. Mel was able to imagine, albeit tenuously, a future, and albeit only an immediate future. Her long range predictions became fuzzy and unclear, like looking through a telescope's damaged lens. None in the trio were prepared to commit to the long term. And research and development of an effectual response to the expanding alia, absent further favorable developments, would be consigned to the long term. Circumstanced as they were, the scientists were constrained to await the encounter between the two forces; one an impersonal force of a foreign nature, the other a force holding within it an alien, but now obviously living, personal life form.

"And the *alia universum* is only one hundred million miles from Earth, but moving toward us at a snail's pace compared to its previous rate. At their respective speeds and courses, the scimitars and the alia will meet in less than one week." Tip added.

The esteemed Dr. Banks had by now become notorious as "the controversial Dr. Banks." She had given no reason, taken no position that was reckless, or not grounded in the best available science. She had done nothing to give just cause for the public at large to debate the prudence of relying on her scientific opinions and conclusions. But IMC had been going after her fang and claw for months now, and the effort had taken its toll. Anytime she was discussed in the media, immediately following there would be air time or print column space given to a critic obliged in some manner to IMC. And at the conclusion of the report, the reader, listener, or viewer, would be left with the option to adopt whichever "opinion" or "allegation" found to be more compatible with one's own predilections, or, as would more often the case, to cynically believe nothing said by anyone.

"And when they do meet, what then?" Mel spoke the unanswerable question that was on everyone's mind. The scant evidence provided but little raw material for their consideration, leaving the three to their own silent musings about what might lie ahead.

. . . .

"We're ruined, Phyllis. IFA is ruined. Every last one of the orbiting satellites, missiles, and thermonuclear warheads are gone according to SPAMDEFCO. Gone! They're so much space debris now, I presume, garbage in LEO." Dickenson W. Ferguson was wailing into Phyllis Winders's video screen in Phyllis's office.

"Not true, Dick. Quite the contrary. Don't you see? What happened up there yesterday was wonderful for IFA. The best." Winders was positively beaming back into Ferguson's video screen in his bedroom at his cushy family residence overlooking the north Atlantic.

"Phyllis, those assets cost billions. Wall Street won't like this at all. We might as well close up shop and open a shoe store, if we can raise the money to do that much."

"Don't worry about Wall Street. Let IMC corporate headquarters calm that storm. They have enough money to prop up IFA surely. Let's do our own part. Just keep calm and listen to me."

"Alright, I'm listening." Ferguson's voice dropped half an octave and became quieter, calmer, per Winder's instruction.

"First, let's review what we know. As you said, all of the military's, or IFA's satellites, missiles and warheads are gone. We can only conclude that the alien spaceships blew them up. We couldn't see anything after they eliminated the observational sats up there. We also know that the alien spacecraft have left as fast as they came; gone away from Earth. Far from a crushing defeat, this will be seen as a resounding victory for Earth, and IFA."

Ferguson was regaining his composure, inch by inch, like a child who has had his boo-boo kissed where it hurt, and a cartoon bandage stuck over it. "How do you figure that, Phyllis?"

"Here is how we're going to do it: 'Yesterday, there was a monumental battle waged in space just outside of Earth's atmosphere between the peace loving Americans on behalf of all Earth, and evil alien beings in highly advanced warships, bent on destroying our planet without provocation from us. In a pitched and costly battle, much of the United States Army's space defense system comprised of cutting edge technology developed by Interstellar Forward Assets were unfortunately destroyed. But the price of victory and the preservation of liberty are never purchased cheaply. And victory there was. After the military's skilled deployment and defensive response to the aliens, the invaders beat a hasty retreat, travelling away from Earth at over 100,000 miles per hour. Earth is saved, thanks to our military and IFA.' Like that?" Phyllis was proud of herself. This one was brewed up in her own head, not by that young upjumper Ellacinda Underwood.

"Hey that sounds great. Yeah, that would do just fine." Ferguson's face on the video displayed a sardonic smile. "I like it."

"At GE, we secure you, don't forget. The president herself is going to broadcast a more flowery version of this counterfactual to the people tonight, prime time. IMC is drafting the monologue for her to read."

"I saw something about her making an address, but I was expecting the worst."

"And Dick, you still haven't heard the best part. Since what happened was a stunning and overwhelming victory for IFA, you now can go back to congress and grab gobs of the stuff, needed, of course, to replenish the military's supplies of thingamajigs, essential to protect our planet. So when you go to Congress next time, take a wheelbarrow for the billions in cash. Oh, and prepare to have both of your butt cheeks kissed."

"Phyllis this will save IFA." Winders knew that. She knew those things. But she didn't know that she had also just saved Dickenson W. Ferguson. During the whole of their video conversation, just off screen on the table next to Ferguson, was a full bottle of barbiturates and loaded semiautomatic handgun.

. . . .

"My fellow Americans, and friends across the world:" President Oberlander began her address to the joint session of congress in somber tones and after waiting a full 45 seconds after the last greeting applause had given way to an expectant silence

"What took place beyond Earth's atmosphere just over 24 hours ago, marked the end of one era, and the dawn of the next. The line we had drawn to defy enemies to cross in our never ending defense of the American people has been moved. That line of defense is now drawn in outer space"

The members of congress, IMC Republicans and WWP Democrats without a single exception, erupted in a riotous standing ovation. After a full minute, order returned.

"America's military and technological might, hitherto unsurpassed in the world, can now fairly be said to be unsurpassed in space."

Another standing ovation from all members ensued, another full minute or longer of riotous applause, despite President Oberlander's humble hand gestures to the members, beseeching them to quiet themselves and be seated.

"We have confirmation, unequivocal confirmation, beyond any dispute, that the alien spacecraft have fled from Earth and are now millions of miles away."

The president was on a roll now. She could have read from a baby crib assembly instruction manual and the members would stand and applaud. But instead what she gave next was the *coup de main* for WWP, IMC, IFA, and the Wall Street that had worried Ferguson.

"But our victory that we deservedly and justly celebrate tonight with thanksgiving, was not purchased cheaply. Much of our space defense systems were destroyed in protecting our planet. That system must be replaced." Oberlander emphasized each word of that last declaration with her fist brought down sharply on the podium. Another standing ovation, and this one lasted longest of all.

"Accordingly, I will seek from you, an increase in defense appropriations commensurate with the cost of replenishing and even upgrading our space defense systems, complete with more assets, more powerful payloads, and newer, updated components." This brought down the house. All members were now on their feet, shouting and clapping. The upper galleries were full and the invited guests were joining in the mania. No two standing in the gallery were happier, giddier, about what the president was saying than Phyllis Winders and Dickenson W. Ferguson.

CHAPTER 37

"Henrietta's latest data would be reassuring were it not for the fact that it is now impossible to wrest a five dollar bill out of congress's hand for anything but militarizing space." Melibea sighed aloud as she lounged on the sofa in her apartment, her back resting against one sofa arm and her legs extended out toward the other end, her ankles and bare feet resting on Tip's trouser legs.

Still, the second universe is only less than six million miles away now, and approaching us, however, barely moving forward at all. Maybe all the brouhaha over building more nukes in space will also slow down in time for us to do something about it." Tip had begun a foot massage for Mel.

"Did you ever hear from Doc T.A. about what Dr. de Rojas's message was?"

"No, she's going to return his call, and let me know after they speak." Mel began playing, now moving one foot onto the sofa cushion and under Tip's near leg, digging her toes into his crotch. "In the meantime. . . ." Mel grinned devilishly. Tip was not slow to respond.

. . . .

Dr. de Rojas's image appeared on Trail's video screen.

"I believe something is soon to happen, Trail. I want to project on your screen what we are watching here." Then Dr. de Rojas switched the image projected from his video screen directly to what the telescope in Cerro Tololo had in view.

Dr. Banks then saw a wide field telescopic lens capture a breathtaking view. The entire background was filled with the blackness of the alia, and in front of the alia, separated from it by perhaps a few hundred thousand miles were the scimitars, perhaps the same that had passed under Earth and proceeded on their way after having scrunched up Earth's offensive pieces of defense into little balls, but a number of them far in excess of those that passed Earth.

"Miqueas, they are many more than we saw when they were here."

"*Sí*, Trail. Thousands. They extend around the concavity of the alia both to the left and to the right as far as we can see. They have been maintaining the same distance from the *alia universum*, moving back at a rate only fast enough to match the slow forward progress of the alia. We cannot say if they are watching, communicating, or preparing to enter or to attack the alia."

"I don't believe they wish to enter it, Miqueas. They could have done that already. It is as if they understand not to allow the alia to reach them." Dr. Banks was mesmerized. "How long have they maintained this status, Miqueas?"

"For nearly one hour they have been." Dr. de Rojas switched away the projected image seen by the telescope, back to his face. *Las cimitarras* have been emanating that same red or orange light from their under prows, the same as we saw when they were visiting us, just before they smashed the satellites and weapons. It was only about fifteen minutes ago the orange under prow lights went dark again."

Mel and Tip were still in bed together, Tip curling his finger around a lock of Mel's hair, when Mel's videophone rang. "That might be Trail. I'll have to take it." Mel left Tip languidly resting in place to find her phone in the next room. She threw on a tee and held the videophone close, avoiding any revealing wide screen appearance on the videophone.

"Hello?"

"Melibea something very exciting is about to happen. I'm watching the scimitars holding their place directly in front of the alia, retreating slowly at a pace equal the alia's slowing advance. Maquias has linked it to my office's video screen in real time. You should come and see this."

"I'm there! Tip! Get dressed and meet me at Trail's office as fast as you can." Mel was in her slacks, shoes, and top, and out the door almost before Tip's feet hit the floor.

Mel and Tip fairly bounded into Dr. Bank's office's reception area. It was a Saturday, and the receptionist was not at work. Dr. Banks had unlocked the outer office door and when she heard Mel and Tip arrive, beckoned them to enter. She didn't want to leave the video screen for a moment. The three watched in rapt silence.

Then, many Earth bound observatories and planetariums besides Cerro Tololo observed the scimitars beginning to change formation from the now familiar and apparently standard traveling formation of the lambda. The 21 scimitar formations began to slowly maneuver the same way they had before destroying the Army's assets. Only this time, rather than only the four interior craft who traveled in the smaller diamond formation within the lambdas, when the lambda opened at the apex, those four assumed a central location in a line formation with the other 17 craft. This maneuver was performed by all formations within sight of Earth, as Dr. de Rojas had explained to Trail.

"The reddish-orange glows are coming back to the front of the craft, brighter than ever!" Tip pointed out what everyone was seeing.

"This could be it, whatever it is." Mel was bug-eyed.

"Trail are you still there?" Dr. de Rojas asked excitedly.

"Yes, I'm here Miqueas."

"Henrietta is detecting far infrared wavelengths from the front under prow lights. The detections range from the Z-band to submillimeter length. Transmission is directed at the alia. From all *las cimitarras,* we see the same.

After about an hour of this assault, there was still no other visible or otherwise detectable change in the relative positions or condition of the alia or the thousands of scimitars, yellow lights from their upper prows, and the reddish-orange from their under prows. The reddish-orange lights continued to transmit the invisible beams, with the far infrared heat byproduct, at the alia, all the while the scimitars continued reversing to maintain the same distance from the alia.

After several minutes of this, Trail and Mel and Tip began to feel restive, and the need to at least stand up and walk a few paces, stretch their arms, touch their toes, restore circulation in their limbs. Then they would sit again and stare.

Tip gallantly offered to walk to the anteroom and retrieve some water for anyone who was thirsty, chancing to miss any unscheduled drama that might occur for the sake of quenching everyone's thirst.

But nothing remarkable happened for an hour, two hours, four hours. The scimitars continued emitting something in the direction of the alia with detectable far infrared heat, and whatever else might be undetectable from Earth or Henrietta, all the while continuing to retreat before the alia's expansion, both forces moving closer and closer to Earth. All agreed that they would take shifts watching the progress of the two forces. Dr. de Rojas would continue providing the real time video of events.

"I'm sorry I sounded a false alarm." Trail apologized. "I hope I didn't cause you to interrupt something important to rush over here for an anticlimax."

"No, don't worry about that a minute. I can afford to miss one climax." Tip's stifled chuckle drew no attention from Dr. Banks. "Tip and I had finished our business together just as you called."

"I can return later to take over the watch, Doc T.A." Tip assured her.

"Thank you, Ernst. Meanwhile, I'll stay on here. Of course, if circumstances warrant, I'll phone again."

CHAPTER 38

"Are you certain Tip, positively certain?!" Dr. Banks was jogging into the planetarium, joining Tip there less than one hour after having left Tip in her office to continue surveillance. Tip yielded the chair to Dr. Banks, and pointed out to her what was being seen by the planetarium's 5.1 meter telescope. Tip had first recalled Mel to watch the drama unfold as between the *alia universum* and the scimitars, and she was on post in Dr. Banks's office.

"I saw it myself in your office on the feed from Cerro Tololo, and I couldn't believe it. So I came here to verify with the university's own telescope. And there it is, Doc T.A. Right there for all to see! A sight for sore eyes!"

"Canopus and Beta Carinae, in constellation Carina. Yes I see them! And look Ernst. There is Epsilon Carinae as well!" Dr. Banks pointed out a third star not mentioned by Ernst.

"I had not noticed Epsilon Carinae, Doc T. A. Yes. I can see it now."

"Where is Melibea, Ernst?"

"She's in your office, monitoring events as we receive them from Chile."

"Some of the stars we can see again for the first time in weeks, or months. Not stars that had been consumed by *alia universum*, but only occluded by the alia, blocked from our view as the alia expanded. We can see them again." Dr. Banks clapped her hands together in happiness.

"And so can just about every amateur astronomer in the south."

"Ernst, the *alia universum* is receding. It is deflating. But how? Why?" Dr. Banks covered her mouth with her hands, and looked into nothing, obviously brainstorming. A ring tone was heard by Tip, but not by Dr. Banks who was still in the initial stages of analysis in her own mind.

"Mel, what is it?"

"The rate of deflation is increasing. The leading edge of the alia is now two light years away from Earth and receding."

"Great. You can tell Doc T.A. yourself. She's here with me." Tip turned the videophone for Mel to impart the new datum to Dr. Banks, that the alia is moving backward faster and faster. Melibea was programming a new search field for the telescope that had been looking at Carina, hoping to see more of her old friends again after a prolonged blackout. Tip then raised the phone to tell Mel "Epsilon Carinae is again visible. Doc T.A. spotted it just now."

And thus as the *alia universum* retreated, more and more of the stars in the southern skies reappeared, after having been blocked from Earth's view for so long by the expanding other universe. The alia's rate of deflation continued to increase, and the astronomical community had been gradually arriving at consensus that it was retreating. But the How question was more problematic for science. Had the alia finally ingested enough matter from our universe to create sufficient positive pressure within it to cause gravitational pull, making the alia collapse? Or, had the scimitars caused the collapse? It was Henrietta herself who had the answer, but only some time later, after her handlers would see the pertinent images she had captured. For when all the military's communication satellites had been smushed by the scimitars, Henrietta was left unmolested. It was if the scimitars recognized her as benign, unequipped to cause harm to anything. And what she had seen and preserved for others to see would amaze.

. . . .

Soon, broadcasters around the world announced the news of the *alia universum's* deflation, and retracing of the steps it had taken to approach so near to Earth's bottom side. As it was heard by listeners to English version low-power news radio in Europe:

A major announcement was made today from Paris by a spokesperson for the International Academy of Astronomy and Astrophysics concerning the threat of the approaching other universe that was discovered a year ago. According to the Academy, the alia universum *has now started to retreat, but the cause of the retreat remains uncertain according to the best available science. The Academy is still investigating possible causes, and is withholding announcement until analysis of further evidence has been made. Whatever the case may prove to be, the alia is now some 2,000 light years away and continuing to rapidly move away from the Earth, at rates exceeding light speed.*

Listeners to International Moderators Corporation, Inc. radio or television broadcasts, or readers of their print media, heard or read this or some variation on the same theme:

The International Academy of Astronomy and Astrophysics, a controversial group of scientists mostly from outside the United States, today placed itself deeper into its self-inflicted imbroglio when it announced, some say hastily, that the intergalactic threat it had contended was about to consume our entire solar system in a short period of time, is now disappearing

Academy scientists, including an elderly Dr. Trailing Arbutus Banks of the United States, had claimed that a bubble of sorts was coming to eat the world. Now they are backpedaling away from that claim, alleging that the bubble they say they saw is backing up. Many other reputable scientists in the field have consistently doubted the spectacular claims of the Academy, even calling the claim a hoax. Critics cite the fact that the Academy's scientists, including Dr. Banks, had earlier used the claim of an encroaching space bubble to seek more funding for itself from Congress.

Now that the Academy's request for taxpayer funding has fallen through in the wake of needed outlay to replenish the space weaponry used to repel the recent all-too-real alien attack, it seems there may never have been any bubble at all.

CHAPTER 39

"I don't suppose the white smocks will return for another request, not anytime soon, Dick." Algernon Amberguese was seeing Dickenson W. Ferguson to the front doors of the GE ground floor after meeting with him on an unrelated matter concerning criticism from WWP cooperating officeholders of IFA's Martian mining operations. Now that IFA had been successfully portrayed as the savior of the world, World Wide Products, Inc., and its co-op offs had adopted a strategy of political guerilla warfare, using small-bore attacks on International Moderators Corporation, LLC, as their new tactic, probing for some weak spot to exploit. Algie and Dickenson's exit conversation had merely drifted to the sublime subject of recent victories, and Algie was enjoying yet another victory lap with one of the secured companies.

"And as for the reason that brought you here today Dick, IFA is so popular now, that I almost feel guilty being paid to inform the public about the goodness of your works. And nowadays our secured members of congress can operate almost entirely on their own in defending any odd criticism of your company It's so easy a child could do it." Algie was a man without a care. His sun shone brighter, his birds sang sweeter, and his food tasted more savory. He felt he could go on forever.

"Good-bye Dick. My best to Maureen and the kids."

"Bye, Algie. Thanks for everything." Algie walked out the door and the first few steps to the outside with Ferguson and breathed in deep drafts of the air that smelled sweeter.

. . . .

"It was the scimitars that destroyed *alia universum*; in much the same way they destroyed the orbiting weaponry we sent to destroy them. Look at these images. Absolutely amazing." Mel was pouring over still prints of video images Henrietta had captured incidental to her other chores. These video images had fortuitously captured real time observations of the scimitars' power to transmit beams or rays of some unknown ability to create a closed atmosphere within a defined area in outer space and then pump enough pressure into that area to cause whatever object was inside to implode. She had also provided us with video images of the crushed satellites and armed missiles being booted out to deep space by the force of the scimitars.

"And then the aliens used the same power against the *alia universum* on a much larger scale, and using thousands more scimitars against the alia." Tip was looking at the same images.

"Similar, but not identical, I would say." Dr. Banks spoke for the first time after seeing the images, and listening to her younger contemporaries expound on the subject. "The scimitars must have two types of related resources on board their spacecraft; one, as you just described, to create enormous artificial pressure within a small confined area, and another to create positive pressure in a massively larger and growing area. That is why when the scimitars undertook the latter mission they used thousands of scimitars, not just a few as they did to destroy Earth's space tools. One method seems to first create an outer shell from the outside and then pump, the other creates positive pressure from within an already enclosed area.

"But I agree with your conclusion that it was the scimitars that caused the demise of the Earth's orbiting weapons and satellites, and the alia. Meanwhile, the *Académie* is releasing all of this new information to the world in the next hour."

CHAPTER 40

Consistent with Dr. Bank's information, the *Académie* dropped its bombshell on the world in the next hour from Paris. A hastily arranged press conference was held at the *Académie*, complete with Henrietta's imagery displaying proof, or what in decades past would have been uniformly accepted as proof, of the twenty-some-odd scimitars peeling away from the main group, glowing reddish-orange from their under prows just before showing the thermonuclear warheads and missiles crumple up into tiny balls and scutter away.

The divided world reacted predictably. Many across the world were alarmed, and concerned that they had been misled to believe that a space battle had resulted in the destruction of the scimitars and the Earth's weapons, but that in the end the scimitars had left. Now it seemed to these people that the scimitars had destroyed Earth's most advanced weapons and then gone about their merry way without having suffered a scratch. Many others, the cynics, cared only that two contending polemical camps had concluded that the threat was gone, and that alone was sufficient for them. They couldn't care less about the Why or the How.

Those in the thrall of IMC explainers and opinionizers were told differently, and they believed differently. Copy was sent out from IMC headquarters, copy that originated in the Guardian Enterprises, LLC's Public Policy Support Unit, largely at the keyboards of Algernon and Ellacinda.

Their counterfactual was spewed by IMC, its subsidiaries, its media and cooperating officeholders throughout America and beyond. That counterfactual fell from the lips of Dickenson W. Ferguson in a number of broadcast interviews he consented to because the interviewers would be friendly, that is, from IMC news outlets with IMC-paid commentators or faux journalists as interviewers. The interview was being broadcast as Dr. Banks, Melibea and Tip were conferring in the planetarium.

"So, Mr. Ferguson, what is going on now with this *Académie* and the little dog-and-pony show they put on from France?" The IMC interviewer, Matthew Atcheson, a middle-aged, jowly, bulging white man, with brown hair graying at the temples, holding a pen in his hand as if it had been surgically implanted there, began the interview. He made sure to emphatically display his best facial sneer and most acidic contempt in his voice when he came to the words "*Académie*," and "France."

Dickenson W. Ferguson, by the time of the interview, had read his printed copy of the version of the IMC/GE prepared counterfactual more than a dozen times, and as recently as five minutes before going on air. It was still in his suit coat pocket as he spoke.

"Mr. Atcheson, we know the source of this slander. It is the same *Académie* that falsely told us about some outer space bubble in an effort to misappropriate taxpayer money for some pet project of theirs. These are the same discredited scientists, and neither they nor the *Académie* should be given any credence. They are really quite beneath contempt."

"Oh, but they say they have irrefutable proof from the Henrietta space telescope. They even showed pictures. What about that?"

"The Henrietta telescope has always been dedicated to the white smock crowd, she is their baby. Of course that telescope is going to show whatever academia or the *Académie* ask it to show." Ferguson had learned his lines well. "The Henrietta is simply not a credible source. Science is simply not a credible source."

"That's a pretty strong indictment, Mr. Ferguson. Are you sure you want to be so forceful?" Atcheson felt comfortable in giving this guy a long leash. This Ferguson fellow had read the same IMC counterfactual Atcheson had read, and was now comfortable that his guest was not going to go off script.

"Yes I do, without hesitation. It would be impossible for me to state IFA's position too forcefully. Let me speak plainly. The scientific community has been lying to the world all along, perpetrating a grand hoax to steal taxpayer money, when the real need had been to fund our military to destroy the aliens in their spacecraft, which IFA hekped to do. And this is the thanks?"

Mr. Ferguson, may I call you Dick?" Ferguson smiled a coquettish smile, and nodded. "Dick, can you stay with us after break? I would like to go into more detail about this French-based *Académie*," more sneer, more contempt, "and one of America's own who sits on its board, a Dr. Trailing Arbutus Banks. We'll be right back." The broadcast went to commercial, advertising various IMC products, services, and public service announcements to raise money for IMC products, services, and cooperating officeholders.

. . . .

Back at the planetarium, Dr. Banks changed the subject.

"And now I have some more news for you two." Mel and Tip broke away from Henrietta's images to look at Dr. Banks. "Henrietta wants us to know that the scimitars have changed course and are on their way towards Earth. Evidently, they would like to pay us a return visit. Only she tells us this time there are roughly twice as many scimitars approaching us. We must have done something the first time to make Earth very popular with them."

"Or very infamous." Mel added.

"You think just maybe we pissed them off when we tried to nuke them?" Tip observed without a hint of irony showing.

"We don't know if those inside the scimitars have emotions. They are so much more intelligent than we are, perhaps if they ever had such feelings they evolved beyond them long ago. I'm unsure why they are coming our way again, but when they were here previously they could have destroyed us, but they only destroyed the missile systems and other military materiel."

"Maybe they were saving their firepower for the alia, and now intend to use the leftovers on us." Mel calculated.

"Perhaps. I assume they will let us know in a few days. That is how long before they arrive.

CHAPTER 41

"God, it's spectacular. It's almost like you're right next to it." The young man peered through the telescope's eyepiece, holding a bottle of beer in one hand and a lit joint in the other.

"Let me look next, please." The woman standing beside him requested. She too had been enjoying libation and smoke on the wooden deck of her friend's remote country cabin.

Those two were only two of the twenty-somethings in the crowd who had gathered there for a night of partying under the scimitars. Alien-watching parties had sprung up across the planet, practically everywhere anyone with a modest telescope or even a powerful pair of binoculars could act as host.

A surprising calm had fallen over the mind of most of the people, removing from them the affliction of panic in the face of some five hundred scimitars parked only about six thousand miles above the surface of Earth, and surrounding it by latitude and longitude. The alien spacecraft had been repelled by SPAMDEFCO when first they came near Earth, and now they had made themistake of coming back for a second helping of defeat, or so went the narrative inculcacted in the minds of most. So many were enthused, rooting for the home team to again answer the insults being delivered by the aliens. The few who were not curious to see and be amazed by the scimitars were more fatalistic, resigned to whatever outcome may transpire. The confidence of everyone in America and beyond had been fed and bucked up to some degree by President Oberlander's latest address from inside the facsimile Oval Office inside the secret Presidential bunker. Her address was a product of Algernon Amberguese, first outlined by him in the corner office of Phyllis Winders with Dickenson W. Ferguson joining the confab on video screen before even the president was told what she was going to read.

"Do you have any weapons that could be used against these aliens Dick? Any at all? Phyllis's facial aspect rarely betrayed lack of self-possession, but at this moment one seeing her would see anything but Woman With Purpose. She was at a loss.

"Phyllis we have no readily available Earth surface weaponry or in LEO. All we have at the present are assets in Low Mars Orbit, and there are a couple of problems with that. One, they are at Mars and cannot be timely repositioned. And two, they are no more protected against some maniac crushing them in outer space than our other missiles were."

Algie completed a wipe down of face, neck and hands, returned his handkerchief to its sleeve, and ventured a thought. "Maybe we don't need any assets this time."

Phyllis, and Dickenson from the video screen, looked at Algie like he had lost his mind under the strain.

"Algie, that, even for us, would be a pretty hard sale. We're going to tell people not to worry, we'll scare away the aliens with Halloween masks?" Phyllis thought her longstanding suspicion that Algernon Amberguese had a screw loose somewhere had been proved at long last to be a low estimate. He must have lost several screws and popped a few rivets as well.

"No, no, no." Algie grinned and slightly chuckled obsequiously, in order to indicate that he took no offense at the abusive sarcasm directed his way from his boss. "What I propose is a counterfactual consistent with the counterfactual we have already produced and disseminated, and which has been working quite well."

"Go on, Algie." Ferguson said.

"We continue to maintain that IFA and the military did drive away the alien spacecraft, and that thanks to the emergency appropriations IFA and the Army sought and received from Congress, and thanks to the industrious and patriotic round-the-clock labor of IFA's corporate management and workers," Algie held out a hand to Ferguson, which was seen by the latter via the video screen, "we have been able to resupply the military's assets in LEO, and we are confident that Earth again will repel the invaders. Like it?"

Phyllis was now certain Algie had taken leave of his senses. "Algie, have you been listening? Dick just said we have no resources, and can't produce them for some time, and even if we could snap our fingers and have them in position today, they would be ineffective."

"Phyllis," Algie was now beginning to feel for the first time in his employment with GE that the tables were turned. He felt in control of a conversation he was having with Phyllis Winders. His pores had gone dormant. Algie was dry as a desert. His handkerchief rested under its sleeve, unneeded. "We tell the people what they need to hear to calm them down, and make them think well of IFA and our cooperating officeholders, including the president herself. The message I just articulated will do all that. Thereafter, one of two things will happen. The aliens will either leave again as they did after their first visit, to do whatever aliens do. In which case, we retell the same story about how IFA saved the Earth, and all of us are on top of the world again. Or. . . . "

"Or, the aliens destroy planet Earth." Ferguson concluded the thought for Algie. "What then?"

"Yes, Dick. Or the aliens destroy Earth. And in that event, no one will be left alive to know we lied." And no one in the room noticed that

Algie had just spoken the one phrase that was prohibited within GE by an unwritten but firm cardinal rule.

"It's all we have." Phyllis concluded. There was nothing more to add, nothing more to do, but give the speech to the president for her to read, and then wait.

. . . .

The White House broadcast cameras and microphones were ready for President Oberlander to begin. Some final touches of make-up were applied to her somber face, and she began to read the statement prepared for her by GE Government Adjunct, Public Policy Support Unit, principally Algernon Amberguese.

"My fellow Americans: Only a short time has passed since Earth, through American leadership, destroyed alien invaders just outside Earth's atmosphere. Now it is my sobering responsibility to come to you again and say 'once more into the breech.' As by now, all have seen and know of the returned presence of the alien spacecraft by the hundreds.

"But I ask you to show the same American resolve and courage that carried the day against these marauders the first time they had the temerity to challenge America's might. Show me that much and we shall prevail.

"The same military weapons systems that defeated the aliens are positioned and at the ready. The resilience of the United States military, SPAMDEFCO, and its civilian contractors, have shown tireless efforts to restore our space defenses with unprecedented alacrity. Our defenses will soon be in position and at the ready. At the appropriate time, I will give, as your Commander-In-Chief, the order to launch our defensive assault. With your help, and the help of Providence, a peace loving Earth shall be restored to tranquility and prosperity, free from all threats.

"Thank you, and good-night." The bright lights were killed. The president removed her microphone, and walked from the replica Oval Office desk and behind the cameras and embraced her husband and children. Then the First Family retired to their undisclosed secured bunker quarters to await the development of circumstances.

CHAPTER 42

The upper prow lights on every scimitar surrounding Earth shone bright yellow above, but the under prow lights, the reddish-orange that had been seen when the scimitars were assaulting the alia, were dark. All scimitars were silent. All were pointed at the Earth, each scimitar a double blade with its two forward points pressed against the world's neck. One conscious decision by one advanced life form made aboard one of the spacecraft, and Earth would collapse, compress to about the size of a small asteroid. All life forms above, on, and below the surface, made extinct in a matter of minutes. Earthlings waited.

"Why don't they *do* something? Hell, why don't *we* do something? What is the president waiting for?" were the answerless questions on everyone's mind, and lips. But in the university's planetarium a different attitude prevailed, one of curious resignation that freed enough thought for theorizing.

"If annihilation were their purpose for returning, they could have done that as soon as they arrived. They've been sitting there for hours now." Melibea spoke first.

"Suppose they have some sort of internal generators that need some time to replenish the pressure forces. They must have expended a lot of energy on the alia. Maybe they're regenerating power in order to launch their assault against us." Tip suggested.

"I'm encouraged by what we *do* know." Dr. Banks, sitting on her cushion on her desk chair, said calmly. "When we saw the scimitars the first time, they were on a straight line course for the *alia universum*, not Earth. I think it safe to say they would not have taken any notice of us had we not posed a thermonuclear threat to them. Before we distracted their attention from their original objective they had, as my grandmother used to say, 'bigger fish to fry.'"

"But the President said we have more nukes in space now, to attack the scimitars." Tip reminded.

"Yes, and she also said the first nuclear missiles had destroyed the scimitars. Henrietta showed us that a much different scene had taken place. Had the military redeployed new thermonuclear assets, we should have seen the scimitars already emitting the pressure beams, but they haven't. If they needed more time to regenerate power to their beams, they would not have approached so close to Earth in the face of capable nuclear missiles, if any nuclear missiles there are."

"And Henrietta has, as of now, seen no nuclear missiles, at least in the areas where she has been told to look." Melibea said.

Dr. Banks seemed uncannily placid, as if her only concerns were which questions to ask, and what information would be relevant to providing their answers. "No, the longer they do nothing, the better it makes me feel."

. . . .

"Hey, take a look. Some of those bastards are gone now!" The man in his twenties called to his fellow partygoers on the roof of the country cabin.

"Are you sure? You didn't jostle the telescope with your elbow again, did you, Robert? How many brews have you had now?" His friend in the tee-shirt and shorts and flip flops, a beer in his hand, sauntered over to the telescope, and Robert moved aside.

"See for yourself. I didn't bump anything." Robert took another toke and another swig as his friend looked into the eyepiece. After a moment he called out.

"Hey, Brenda, come here! I think some of the aliens have left. There're still most of them, but I think a few have left." The flip flops flip-flopped aside for Brenda. She bent at the waist to peer through the eyepiece, joint between her fingers, and holding her Tom Collins in the other hand.

"They've moved somewhere, or maybe the good guys shot them down. But some are not there anymore. Did anybody see any, like, explosions?" Brenda eagerly looked up and around.

Twenty-four hours after the 525 scimitars took positions surrounding the Earth from pole to pole, some were pulling up stakes and leaving.

. . . .

"They're beginning to leave in squadrons of five formations each, in the usual lambda formation of 21 craft. The first squadron left two hours ago on a course retracing the path that brought it so near to Earth when they arrived, just before proceeding to the *alia universum*." Melibea felt an adrenalin rush from the spectacular events that were now unfolding after hours of tedium spent waiting and watching nothing change.

"Yep. Now a second squadron has broken away and is following after the first on the same course and speed. That's. . . . 210 scimitars gone, 315 remaining parked just outside of Earth." Tip completed the account up to the minute.

Melibea and Tip and, of course Dr. Banks, had never left the planetarium since the scimitars first besieged Earth. Tip had brought in his and Mel's sleeping bags they kept stowed under the bed for use on camping trips, and he had borrowed a cot for Dr. Banks to curl up in so each of them could catch a cat nap while at least one watched for developments. Now, late in the evening, they were looking through the planetarium's own telescopes. So near to Earth were the alien spacecraft that Henrietta's and Cerro Tololo's valuable assistance were needed only to see beyond the planetarium's telescopes' own field of view. The scimitars directly above America were easily seen by even the smallest of the university telescopes.

"Trail. Trail." Mel gently rocked Dr. Banks's left shoulder as the latter dozed on the cot after having watched the scimitars, virtually without blinking, for hours. After the first squadron of five departed and things were quiet again for nearly two hours, Dr. Banks decided to give her eyes a rest. But she was not in deep sleep, and immediately responded to Melibea's gentle prodding.

"Yes, Mel. I'm awake. What is happening?" Dr. Banks said clearly as she raised herself from the cot and put her small feet into their slippers.

"A second squadron of five scimitars is leaving. Two hours after the first we saw."

"A pattern developing? Too soon to say? I must look. What were the locations of the two squadrons that left us?" Always the scientist, always raising more questions from the new answers, Dr. Trailing Arbutus Banks was up, fresh as a daisy, gathering information and data to feed into her inquisitive, never sleeping mind. This was her kind of fun.

By late the next morning, within forty-eight hours of their laying siege to Earth, all the scimitars had left the vicinity, and were headed on a course from whence they came, at a high rate of speed, disappearing again into the cosmos. They had not sent a single beam, not emitted a single blast of any force of destruction down to the planet that had sent its thermonuclear missiles to destroy them. They had watched, assessed, and then left.

. . . .

"Let us rejoice and give thanks as we have been delivered from those who would have done harm to peace loving humankind." President Oberlander was returned to the actual White House a few hours after final confirmation that the scimitars had indeed parted from our company. She was in fine form addressing a televised audience from the Rose Garden. She was standing in front of her family, cabinet members, Congressional leadership, the Military Joint Chief of Staff, Chief of Staff of SPAMDEFCO, and others who had wedged themselves onto the fringes of the Presidential backdrop.

Everyone in the group of dignitaries attending the president knew what they had chosen to know happened in the space above Earth. That is to say they had been credulous when told what was so by IMC and WWP science experts. What they consequently knew was that the aliens had blinked. The peace loving humans had aimed their mighty weapons at the alien spacecrafts, but then had held their fire. The aliens, recognizing the hopelessness of the odds arrayed against them, and the folly of trying to contend against so massive a force as that being directed against them by SPAMDEFCO, had thrown in the towel, and ran home, tail between their legs, cravenly defeated without firing a shot.

That counterfactual narrative, provided by IMC and WWP feeders, pleased the ears of the president and all those in government down the line to Sgt. Stannis and the White House interns. The narrative was pleasing to them and accepted wholly by them because it affirmed their wish for it to be true, a wish that arose after investing so much time, treasure and emotion, into making it become true. That the narrative had no correspondence to reality was to them a proposition worthy of consideration only to be refuted as some false, baneful, accusations being made by those with ulterior motives, or pitiful innocents who had been duped.

"We in government would be remiss if we did not take this opportunity to recognize our unequaled military and especially our Army's Space

Military Defense Command. General Paterson," the President turned to her right, "your nation thanks you."

. . . .

"Ellacinda, I want you to work with Jerry and Algie to maximize the benefit to be derived from the defeat of the aliens at the hands of the Interstellar Forward Assets' whirligigs. We must strike while the iron's hot. We have no excuse if we do not do for our co-op offs enough to insure majorities in every legislative body, and seats in every governor's mansion across the country in the next election cycle." Phyllis's demeanor had returned to its usual texture, calm and in total command and control. Algie listened respectfully, but he would always have his moment in the sun to reminisce. He had provided the counterfactual that had pulled GE out of the fire, and what is more, had calmed America, and the world for that matter, when the alternative would have been mass panic in the streets, and an unraveling of all civilized self-restraint. When all others around him were wailing and gnashing their teeth, Algernon Amberguese knew it was he who had stepped into the breech, not Phyllis Winders, not SPAMDEFCO, and not President Oberlander.

"So step lively. We need these feeds to begin going out to the cooperating officeholders and our media outlets today. Thank you all." Phyllis, in the wake of the crisis and its happy ending, had developed a verbal tic of saying "Thank you" to announce to her auditors that she had concluded. Her minions left the room and scurried to their stations to begin creating the needful, weaponized facts to help America understand and appreciate, and be secured.

. . . .

Some months later, Dr. Banks paid a visit to Dr. de Rojas in Chile. They did dine at *La Cocina Selena*, and partook of the *chapaleles*. Mamacita was gracious and elated to see *La Flor de las Sierras*, or simply *La Flor* as she called Trail, in reference to Dr. Bank's namesake.

As they turned their eyes and forks to a small plate of *pasteles* for dessert, the table conversation turned to science.

"As we discussed on the videophone Trail, we are gradually seeing more and more bodies pass into areas formerly occupied by *alia universum*. And that is a happy event."

"Yes, Miqueas. That is the truth. Not only are we seeing stars and clusters that existed before being occluded by the alia, we now can see other bodies whose natural orbits and movements have impelled them into the empty areas where the alia had consumed all in its path."

"And those appear to be unaltered by their entrance into those areas. Another happy event." Dr. de Rojas pushed away his emptied plate of *pasteles*.

"*Otros pasteles más, Miqueas? Flor?*" Mamacita amiably offered them.

"*No, gracias, Mamacita. Fueron muy sabroso.*

"*No, gracias. Son deliciosos.*

"So, a new normal begins to take shape. We will have to begin remapping the heavens all over again." Dr. Banks noted.

"Yes my friend. We are the new beginners, making the first star charts of *los cielos nuevos.*

And so it became that when astronomers viewed the southern quadrants, they no longer were seeing a dark region occupied by an advancing excrescence, eating all before it. A new normal had indeed begun to emerge, one that would evolve over millennia, over eons, giving light and form to a dark emptiness within a universe that the alia had left behind.

EPILOGUE

In the Astronomy Department's meeting room Dr. Banks, Mel, Tip, and other members of the university's Department of Astronomy and Astrophysics, sat in a group discussing how they could now continue researching into these phenomena: the second universe and its apparent demise, and the appearance and withdrawal of the extraterrestrial life in the scimitars. Some of the apostate members of Mel's original supernova search team had contritely returned, seeking to atone, now that it was safe to go back into the skies. They were welcomed.

Melibea listened to all this for some minutes, entering her own incisive comments and relevant questions here and there, before the intriguing conversation began to lose some of its luster for her, and her mind began to wander. Her eyes, not her scientific eyes, caught sight of beauty through the window to the outdoors. She saw the last pale pink of nature's paint dripping down into the far off horizon of the western sky, and the brightening light of Venus, the misnamed "Evening Star." It was still there; such an obviously banal, but for her now a profound and moving, thought. Much, Melibea considered, was *still there*. For all that had been taken, much remained.

As her spiritual and philosophical side mused on the sunset, Mel recalled from her undergraduate days the Buddhist teaching that all phenomena are inherently transitory, empty of any unchanging permanence, dependent on originating causes to bring them into being, and ultimately destined to undergo the changes that will remove them from being. In Mel's estimation, all of that had happened, and would ever continue to happen.

Indeed, much would continue to happen in Melibea Paz's immediate orbit in the next several years; another banal yet profound thought. Life *would* happen. Lives would continue in ways that Melibea could not know or predict—but they *would* continue.

Dr. Trailing Arbutus Banks would begin immediately to gather together her research on the phenomenon of the other universe, and writing of a treatise on the subject. That effort had begun at the dining table at *La Cocina Selena.* Her reputation, and that of many other astronomers, astrophysicists and cosmologists, had been refurbished to their original brilliance in the wake of a revision in the mind of many people, who were beginning to dare to think that the white smock crowd had been at least partially correct all along.

The project of the treatise she pursued on and off for another nine years, with the publishing of the first volume, and commencement of the concluding second volume. Melibea was there helping her, of course. After Dr. Banks's macular degeneration progressed so far, Melibea would also be her reader of everything needful that had not been recorded. Dr. Banks held onto the helm of the Department she had loved and raised into pre-eminence for as long as she could, but then gave way, to devote herself entirely to her treatise. She would not complete its second volume before her health failed her, and the stardust that was Trailing Arbutus Banks transitioned into its next phase. Mel would complete the treatise as a Ph.D. in Astronomy and Astrophysics, and eventually ascend to the Chair of that Department at the university. IMC's ability to influence hiring decisions in academia had waned somewhat, after the episodes with the alia and the scimitars. Many still believed the corporate version, but enough persons in enough universities stiffened against the forces that would not allow studies to develop cramped within constraints of considerations of monetary gain.

When Mel became Chair of the Department, she returned Trail's desk and the hickory fanback chair that Trail had bequeathed to her, and situated them in their former places in the office, Trail's office as Melibea would always regard it. Mel's physical stature didn't require her to use the seat cushion, so Mel displayed it alongside a portrait of Dr. Banks, on top of a bookcase in the office, above everything else in the room.

Phyllis Winders would take early and wealthy retirement from Guardian Enterprises, LLC, after another five years. She and her new bride would move to their 200-acre piece of prime real estate, north of Vancouver, BC, and there they would do, well, anything they wanted to do.

Algernon Amberguese would be promoted from within GE ranks, and in turn Ellacinda Underwood would be promoted to head the Public Policy Support Unit. And IMC and GE and WWP would continue to manage, support and direct their cooperating officeholders as they always had. And IMC and WWP would continue their aged competition against one another, like arm wrestlers of mythological strength, neither able to push the other's arm all the way down.

Dickenson W. Ferguson would survive the scimitars' second visitation on Earth by less than a year. He would be killed on the moon, during an inspection visit to IFA's ongoing installation of a relay station launch facility to Mars. He had just completed an inspection of the base and had stepped into a faulty air lock, and removed his space suit helmet when it was supposedly safe to do so. His head exploded its contents all over the air lock that had killed him. Dickenson W. Ferguson had worn his homburg for the last time.

Carlton Hindman retired from the House and politics two years later. As popular as ever with the home folks, no opponent having ever ran closer to him than 17 points. He and his wife of 52 years, Verla, lived on their small ranch in the hill country. When the little Texas tornado blew out for the last time, he was laid to rest on a hill beneath a small grove of blackjack oak and chickasaw plum trees on the ranch. Verla planted a white rose bush on either side of his, of course, oversized, headstone. The first white rose bushes she planted on Carlton didn't take well. They died despite Verla's best efforts. But a multiple blue ribbon winner is not daunted by minor setbacks, and she replanted a second brace of her roses. This time she admonished Carlton, "Now Carlton, you leave these roses alone, and let me tend to them this time. You know you don't do it the right way." And her Carlton must have listened to Verla, for the second pair of bushes thrived, and grew in a size to rival the headstone. They produced so many beautiful white blossoms that no one coming to visit the late congressman had any trouble finding him.

Dr. Miqueas de Rojas, "the dear," would in time ascend to the Chair of the *Académie internationale de physique et d'astronomie*, where he would further distinguish himself in the field of astrophysics and cosmology. It had for Dr. de Rojas the added personal benefit of facilitating more frequent visits to see his relatives in the Old Country; Malaga, Spain being only a comparatively small jaunt from Paris.

As for *Bubbly Effervescence and the Cork Poppers,* the show would go on, but with a new Bubbly. Tony Goodman decided to concentrate on performing in the church choir, and exclusively as Tony Goodman. No one other than a few, not including his wife, would ever know that he had been a successful stage performer.

The police would finally commit Max's murder to the cold case files. No significant leads would ever materialize. But Melibea still knew. She thought of Max now and again. She would always think of him now and then. She had learned from Max. The sharp, biting edges of her social outlook had been smoothed. She would still care about the things she always cared about, but she had learned to sometimes let go, to put things in their proper perspective and prioritize them within the context of her own personal life.

Nor could Mel know that her own personal life in two years would absolutely rearrange her priorities. After the worldwide upheavals had subsided and Mel and Tip had been together for more than a year, as friends and lovers, they were on a camping trip together high in the Rocky Mountains. They had hiked to a camping spot as high as they could find to be cool enough in the summer. The tree line had gradually risen to elevations where trees had not been able to thrive in past decades, and Mel and Tip set up camp amid small clusters of evergreens. They were lying supine next to each other on their blankets with a light blanket on top of them. The campfire had ebbed to embers and a few, small, licking flames. Tip was holding Mel close to him, her head resting on his shoulder. And they were gazing at the stars, naturally. But what worried Melibea was Mel's unusual silence. He had become eerily quiet for her big brown haired chatterbox. And then as a meteor blazed across their line of sight Mel started, and exclaimed on its beauty. And at that Tip broke his silence. He told her that he had found the most beautiful binary system in the entire universe, and that he would be the happiest man alive if he lived to never see it explode. Mel raised up, excited, and said he should have told her before, and asked him where is it, in which galaxy. And Tip said it was in an out-of-the-way spiral of the Milky Way, on planet Earth, lying on a blanket in the Rockies, and then he kissed her. The next morning they broke camp and started down the mountain, together, as they would be always. Three years later, with a little help from medical science, Melibea was delivered of a healthy little boy. They named him Johannes, after the famous German astronomer Johannes Kepler. When Johannes was six, his parents gave him his first starter telescope and set it up for him one night to see the moon.

"But I can see the moon. There it is." Johannes correctly pointed it out to his ignorant parents.

"But with a telescope you can see it up close. Look." Tip showed him how to look through the telescope, and then let him try.

Mel and Tip watched him, hoping for an awe-inspired "Wow!" or other precocious comment about the Earth's only natural satellite. But instead what they received was "But it doesn't do anything. May I go back inside and play with my toys now?" So Johannes went inside and played with his battery operated pieces of molded plastic that moved and made noises, and an astronomy career was deferred, at least temporarily.

But none of this could Melibea know as she drifted in and out of the group conversation in the department conference room, and as she watched more and more stars come out against the darkening night to adorn Venus.

She wondered if the *alia universum's* ingestion of our universe's matter had had any effect on the slowing of the other universe's acceleration prior to the aliens destroying it. It had slowed before the fleet visible to Earth had begun its assault, but she knew there had been at least a few hundred, maybe thousands, of other fleets of scimitars approaching from unseen areas that had commenced the assault earlier. Those additional scimitars had visited Earth on their return trip home. Had the original approaching fleet only joined in as a mopping up operation?

And Melibea wondered about the aliens that had apparently destroyed the other universe. She wondered if we should continue regarding them as aliens at all. They were now to be regarded as inhabitants of *our own* universe. That sounded strange to her. But now those visitors were life forms in *our own*, as opposed to *the only* universe. Other universes were no longer merely hypothetical. We had witnessed one such *alia universum*, and that meant there could be more. That thought made our universe seem to shrink, to become smaller and more intimate. The universe that those inside the scimitars had saved was, after all, our shared universe—the scimitars' and ours. They were our neighbors, and it was our mutual interest they had protected.

Of course, Mel knew that the aliens did not travel all the way from wherever they came to visit Earth for any reason—beneficent, benign or malignant—it was a chance encounter when the alien sojourners were on their way to somewhere else. She also knew that in destroying the other universe the aliens weren't acting altruistically to save us, surely. They might have never even known we exist if we had not tried our space weapons on them. After they had scrunched our puny missiles and threw them away, they went on to their business at hand. They returned to Earth only to assemble and briefly observe us for a couple rotations of our planet. After taking our measure they had seemed to say "Meh," and began the voyage back to their inhabited home planets and moons, not considering us worth the powder it would take to blow our ass to hell.

She wondered if we should try to contact them. Begin sending radio waves in the direction whence they had come, prefaced by a sincere apology. And what if they did receive our communication? Would they be impressed or even mildly curious? She wondered if they would simply pass our sincere greetings around to each other and have a good laugh at our expense, a chuckle over how some primitives light years away had squeaked at them.

The southern skies had been emptied by the alien universe's progression and then retreat, like a gargantuan intergalactic glacier had scoured the skies and then receded, leaving them bare, gone, forever. The alien universe's energy had devoured all in its path. In time, long after Melibea and anyone else alive with her would be alive to see it, with the expansion of our universe, and the movement of the remaining stars and planets, asteroids and comets, those areas would again be filled, and provide a sight reminiscent of the olden eons. As Drs. Banks, Paz, and de Rojas knew, eventually there would be a return to normalcy, not the old normal, but a new normal.

Centuries from now, astronomers yet unborn would find stellar arrangements in those areas, and give them names of objects, real or mythical, that the arrangements would evoke in the minds of their Earthly beholders. And perhaps our yet unknown neighbors on other planets would do the same.

Eventually, the rest of the astronomers departed the room where the recent conference was gathered, but Mel stayed. No one thought that unusual; Melibea was often the last to leave at night.

As the sky darkened to a cobalt blue hosting some gray, scudding, broken cloud cover, Mel wondered if musing upon the Evening Star would yield up to her answers to the new question of how she should proceed now. Go back to searching for a supernova, after all this? Most of PG6240 was still there. When the *alia universum* had explosively transitioned it had not performed in the same way as our own universe had in the Big Bang. *Alia universum* had expanded not in every direction spherically, but outward toward our galaxy, and then widening after that, more like a teardrop shape. The White Rose had lost only its one petal. Melibea wondered if she would now find searching through spectrographic data boring, that the effort would suffer by comparison to what she had just been through. She certainly had another option to searching for SNs. There was enough raw material left by the alia and the scimitars to be studied by every astrophysicist and cosmologist on Earth for decades, centuries to come. What would she do now?

Dr. Melibea Paz looked at the stars and wondered if *las cimitarras* would ever return. . . . .she looked at the stars and wondered if. . . .she wondered.

THE END